I0598530

Bride of Regret

Brides By Mail
Book Three

By

Cami Wesley
& Amanda Tru

Published by
Walker Hammond Publishers

Walker Hammond

Publishers

PUBLISHED BY: Walker Hammond Publishers

Some scripture quotations courtesy of the 1611 King James Version (KJV) of the Holy Bible.

Some scripture quotations courtesy of the New King James Version (NKJV) of the Holy Bible, Copyright© 1979, 1980, 1982 by Thomas-Nelson, Inc. Used by permission. All rights reserved.

Original Cover Art by Debi Warford (www.debiwarford.com)

Library Cataloging Data

Tru, Amanda (Amanda Tru) 1978-
Wesley, Cami (Cami Wesley) 1981-
   Bride of Regret/Cami Wesley and Amanda Tru
     198 p. 20.32cm x 12.7cm (8in x 5in.)

Summary:Humorous episodes on a 19th century Texas ranch make a man rethink his regrets and a woman wish she was another man's mail-order bride.

Identifiers: ISBN-13: 978-1-68190-042-1 (trade) | ISBN-13: 978-1-68190-041-4 (Print on Demand) | ISBN-13: 978-1-68190-040-7 9 (ebook)

1. Western 2. Mail Order Bride 3. Traditional Romance 4. male and female relationships 5. Christian Inspiration

[PS3568.AW475 M328 2016]
248.8'43 — dc211

Bride of Regret

Brides By Mail
Book Three

By

Cami Wesley & Amanda Tru

Table of Contents

Prologue

Pete

Bar H Ranch,
Last Chance, Texas–1879

"Pete, she's asking for you."

Pete stood still, longing to completely ignore Josh's words and run away as he had over twenty years ago. But he'd taken the coward's way out then, and as much as he wanted to, he couldn't do the same now.

Pete nodded and wordlessly turned to climb the stairs.

"Pete?"

Josh's hoarse voice stopped him.

"Pete, she isn't going to make it."

Pete felt his jaw flex with tension. Unfortunately, he had no words of comfort, neither for Josh, nor himself.

Resolutely, he walked the rest of the way up the stairs, trying not to think or feel. He mechanically opened the door. Hopefully, he could make an appearance and escape before his armor cracked and his emotions won.

Quietly, he approached her bed. Her eyes were closed, and Pete watched the slow, almost imperceptible rise and fall of her chest as she breathed. She was sleeping, and he wouldn't disturb her.

His eyes were irresistibly drawn to her face, and he allowed himself to study her features, something he hadn't permitted himself in the last twenty years. He was an expert at looking past her, never meeting her eyes. But, now, with no one to notice, his gaze traced the features of the face he had loved.

She was pale, her dark hair standing in stark contrast to her pallor. She'd always been fair, and even now, though a few fine lines marked her otherwise smooth face, not a trace of gray marred her hair. But why should it? She was still young. Jake had been gone for over ten years, and yet she had raised Josh herself, with minimal help from her brute of a brother-in-law who wouldn't even look at her.

And unfortunately, he was that brute of a brother-in-law.

She should have remarried.

She should have married him.

Pete's throat burned. He struggled to swallow and keep down the emotion. Maybe things would have been different if he'd let go of his anger and pride. If he hadn't let bitterness consume him, maybe she wouldn't be lying in this bed right now.

Pete had lost his brother, and now he was losing her. He

should have learned after Jake, and yet, for over twenty years he never met the eyes of the one woman he loved. Never spoke what needed to be said. And now…

Pete gasped, no longer able to stop the tears. "Isobel, please don't leave!"

Isobel's eyes remained closed, and yet Pete's mind immediately jumped back to when those same words were spoken to him well over twenty years ago. Despite the pain, his mind replayed the scene as if it was being acted out in front of him.

"Pete, please don't leave." His older brother's gaze was dark with turmoil.

"She chose you, Jake," Pete answered, his tone clipped and devoid of any of the emotion evident in his brother's eyes.

"It doesn't have to be this way," Jake agonized. "You don't have to go."

"I can't stay here and see you two together," Pete said, shaking his head as he cinched the strap on his saddle tighter. "Don't you see that?"

"You're young," Jake pleaded. "You're eighteen-years-old. You might feel differently later."

Pete grit his teeth, trying to push down the anger. Fearful his fury would get the best of him if he actually looked at Jake, he continued adjusting the saddle and flung the words over his shoulder. "I love her, Jake, just as much as you do. You might be four years older, but you have never treated me like a child. So don't you start now."

"I'm sorry, Pete," Jake said, chagrined. He raked his fingers through his dark hair, desperation in his every movement. "I didn't mean to make light of your feelings. I just don't want you to leave like this. This ranch is what we worked for, what we've dreamed of. Pete, you're all the family I have left."

Pete swallowed the lump that formed in his throat. Gazing off into the distance, he took a few moments before responding softly, "You will build a new family. With Isobel. You don't need me anymore."

Jake grabbed Pete by the shoulders and gripped him tightly, his fingers digging in painfully. "You are my brother! I will always need you!"

Pete shrugged Jake off and stepped back, crossing his arms as if to shield himself.

Jake, seeing he was getting nowhere, tried a different tactic. "Look around," he gestured. "This is our ranch. The Bar H belongs to you just as much as it does to me. I know you are angry and hurt, but we've worked too hard—you've worked too hard—to walk away from this ranch now. I know you. You will regret it if you leave. Ranching is in your blood. Don't give up on our dream now. We can make this work. I won't lose you."

Pete studied the ground for several heartbeats. Then he slowly put his foot in the stirrup and swung himself into the saddle. Looking down at his brother, he stared straight into his eyes and said, "You're right. I will have regrets. I do already. You want to know what I regret the most? I regret that a woman ever set foot on this ranch."

Pete shut his eyes, once again hearing the last words he had ever spoken to his brother. How they had echoed through his mind over the years, torturing him with the remembrance and shame.

And now, the woman who drove them apart, lay on the bed, with her heart likely beating its last. And he had no more words for her than he'd had for his brother. He may even have less. Over twenty years of bitterness had built a large wall.

"Pete."

Isobel's soft voice pulled him from his memories. His eyes flew open.

With a gentle smile on her face, Isobel Harding reached a weak hand to him.

Pete automatically grasped her fingers, struggling to find something—anything—to say.

"Thank you," Isobel said first.

Pete's eyebrows rose in shock. Why in the world would she be thanking him? "For what?" he asked incredulously.

"For stepping in and teaching Josh about ranching. For being the dad he needed when we lost Jake."

Pete swallowed. "It wasn't enough." He met her eyes, seeing the same pain reflected in her. Oh, how he'd loved her! Even after all these years, after so much hurt, his heart beat for her.

"I'm sorry to ask you this, Pete, but I need you to take care of him," Moisture gathered in Isobel's eyes as she spoke. "I know he's a grown man, and I don't deserve any kindness from you. But Josh needs you."

Pete nodded. "Consider it done." Despite everything, he would not leave his nephew the way he had his brother.

Isobel wet her lips and struggled to speak. "Pete, I'm sorry. For everything."

A sob caught in Pete's throat, and tears trailed down his cheeks. "No, Isobel, I'm the one who should..." Pete struggled. How do you communicate twenty years of regret?

He looked at Isobel, hiding none of the raw emotion. Pete had the awful feeling that no words could make recompense for his sins. He couldn't think of anything he could say that would both convey his remorse and speak of how much he still cared.

If he could have done things differently…

Finally, he spoke in a helpless, strangled whisper, "Isobel, I don't know how to do this."

Isobel sighed and gently squeezed his hand. "Pete, you don't have to say anything. You never realized how much I cared for you, how much I always have. A few years after Jake passed, I wondered if you would ever forgive me. If maybe you and I… but then a few years turned into ten. Josh was twelve when Jake died, and now he's grown. I guess we had too much past hurt, enough that more than twenty years couldn't forgive."

"I don't think forgiveness was ever the issue for me," Pete rasped out, feeling sorrow rip through him. Had his pride kept him from happiness all these years? "I've always cared for you. That didn't stop. But I never wanted to be your second choice."

Isobel sighed. "Just because I chose Jake didn't mean that you didn't have a place in my heart. Pete, you would have never been second to anyone. Maybe if I was a better, a bolder woman, maybe I would have explained how I felt. I shouldn't have let this wall stand between us all these years. Jake wouldn't have wanted it that way, even if you are as prickly as a cactus!"

Isobel's words only increased Pete's guilt. It had been his fault. She shouldn't take any responsibility at all. She had followed her heart, lost her husband, and faced years of Pete's resentment, yet she had always returned his hateful actions with kindness. Even after her health began to decline and she was in constant pain, she'd only ever been sweet to him.

Pete swallowed with difficulty. He knew what he needed to say. But it was both the most simple and most difficult petition he had ever made. "Isobel, please forgive—"

As if on cue, Isobel's body was racked with coughing. Pete watched helplessly as she struggled to breathe and her face gradually gained a bluish tinge. He longed to call for the doctor, but he knew that the medical field had already done all it could. Not knowing what else to do, Pete helped her sit up, praying that she would capture that next breath.

Josh rushed into the room, hurrying to his mother's side. Gradually her coughing subsided, and she fell back to the bed, her breathing shallow and her color gray.

Pete bent down and reverently placed a kiss on her forehead. Then he backed up, letting Isobel's son have the place he deserved.

As Josh prayed and spoke words of love to his mother, Pete slipped back out the door.

He knew this was the last time he would ever see Isobel this side of heaven, and yet he felt he hadn't handled that goodbye any better than the one with his brother.

Overwhelmed and unable to go on, Pete let his forehead fall against the wall as he leaned against it for support. In a way, the last beat of Isobel's heart would mark the last beat of his. With her would die all hope for love and redemption.

And he had no one to blame but himself.

For the first time in a long time, Pete cried out to God, begging for a forgiveness he knew he didn't deserve. But somehow, making things right with his Lord didn't erase the consuming regret.

Women didn't belong on ranches, and he would forever carry the reminder. For he knew, as if he'd just been given a life sentence, that he would always be haunted with regret over the one woman who would never leave his heart.

 # Chapter 1

JO

Near Last Chance, Texas –1881

"Are you alright? Did we hit something?"

Terrified screams pierced the darkness as Jo struggled to regain consciousness. "What happened?" she mumbled confusedly.

Sharp pain radiated from a spot on her temple. With gentle fingers, she found the round swelling of a large goose-egg. She must have hit her head. But how? Where was she?

Chaotic blurs of light danced across her vision. She had been on a train, traveling at night. She must have nodded off in her seat with her head against the window. Only now, she awoke in the pitch black with the frantic cries of frightened passengers.

Why had the train stopped so suddenly? And why were there no lights?

"Jo, are you there? Are you alright?" A voice called from slightly above her. Meg. Jo had been seated next to her.

"I'm fine," Jo said, struggling to sit up. But the second she moved, sharp pain shot through her ribs. She sucked in her breath and shut her eyes, waiting for the pain to subside.

"Where are you?" Meg asked worriedly. "Have you seen any of the other ladies?"

Jo breathed out slowly and tried to keep the pain from her voice as she spoke. "I think I'm on the floor. Or the ceiling. I can't be sure which direction is up." Obviously, if she didn't know where she was, she couldn't have seen anyone else. Not bothering to answer that question, Jo flung back one of her own. "Where are you?"

A kick from a pointed boot to the center of her back, sent Jo to her hands and knees, gasping. The force of the blow shot through to her ribs, and it was several seconds before she could grit out. "Floor! Definitely the floor. I'm beneath your feet."

"Oh, sorry!" Meg apologized. "It's so dark. I can't see a thing!"

"Clearly," came Jo's muffled reply.

"Ladies and gentlemen, if I can have your attention," a man's voice called from the front of the rail car.

That must be the conductor, Jo thought, batting at the air around her until she located the seat. Gingerly, she dragged herself up onto the cushion.

"We seem to have hit something that was on the tracks.

The train is off the rails, but we don't believe there are any serious injuries or cause for alarm. Please do not panic. However, there is some concern that this car is in danger of tipping over. We will be moving all of you to a different train car farther down the line until assistance arrives from Last Chance. If you are able to, gather your belongings, and exit to the front."

"Where is the front exactly?" A man yelled from behind Jo. "It's darker than the inside of a cow in here!"

"Well, that answers one of my questions. We are most certainly in Texas," Jo whispered to Meg as the other woman finally plopped down onto the bench next to her.

"Shh," Meg hushed her. "The conductor is speaking."

Jo shook her head. It was nice to see that the crash hadn't injured Meg at all. She was still the consummate rule-follower.

"We are trying to locate lanterns and candles," the conductor continued. "Please do the best you can. If you are injured, please remain where you are until we can assist you."

"Can you find your bag?" Meg asked, her voice muffled.

Jo felt her wiggling movements as Meg bent to check the space beneath their seat. "I can't seem to find mine. Oh, wait! I think I just found it."

Jo felt a tug near the hem of her skirt. "No. That's my dress."

"Oh, sorry."

"I can tell you from first-hand experience, our bags are not in front of the seat," Jo informed, not sure how much more jostling she could take from Meg's search. "They must have been shuffled when the train stopped suddenly. We really have little hope of finding them right now. Let's just try to get off the train and find the others."

At Meg's agreement, Jo carefully lifted herself from the seat. Trying to steel herself against the pain while keeping her upper body as still as possible, Jo led the way as they slowly crept toward what she hoped was the front of the train.

Moments later, a match flickered in the darkness, and the conductor's face became visible in the light from the lantern he held aloft. "Ladies, let me assist you down the steps," he offered.

"Thank you, sir," Jo replied.

Grasping the man's hand for support, she tentatively felt for the edge of the first step with the tip of her boot. But the instant her head entered the open air, a sheet of water poured over it. It was raining. And apparently this wasn't the type of rain Jo was accustomed to. It was a Texas rain.

It didn't really fall in drops, but was as if God was in the clouds rapidly priming the handles of a million, highly effective hand pumps to produce steady streams of water. Also, strange was the fact that the rain wasn't at all cold. It seemed almost wrong to be so warm in the black of night; and the rain, instead of bringing relief, only increased the discomfort.

Four steps more and Jo was completely soaked, yet on solid ground. Well, not quite solid. The ground in Texas felt oddly squishy, and her boots made sucking noises as she lifted them to walk farther from the train.

"What is that smell?" Meg asked as she stumbled off of the train behind Jo.

"Careful! I'm right—"

Jo landed on her hands and knees, yet again, with Meg on top of her. "—in front of you." Jo gasped at the throbbing radiating from her ribs. Thankfully, the ground was so soft that the landing was not a hard one. It could have been much worse.

"Sorry!" Meg exclaimed, quickly shifting her weight off Jo and scrambling to her feet. "I couldn't see you! It's so dark. I can barely see my hand in front of my face. Where are the lanterns?"

When Jo still didn't move after being relieved of her burden, Meg hesitantly asked, "Are you hurt? Do you need help up?"

"No, I'm fine," Jo replied, her tone clipped. She carefully struggled upright. Every movement caused more pain and discomfort. It didn't help that her boots continued to slip in the muddy terrain, and her hands were coated with the thick sludge. It must be dripping from everywhere, even her hair.

Jo strained her eyes, trying to figure out where they were supposed to go now. She saw the dark shadow of the conductor urging passengers along the line, and she lifted up her boots in high steps, trying to quickly follow.

Meg moaned. "There is so much mud here! Perhaps there was a mud slide that washed out the tracks? This rain is awful, and the conductor mentioned that it has been raining a lot." Meg stomped her boots, trying to dislodge the muck.

Jo figured her boots were a lost cause, and simply trudged forward. But her hands were different. She couldn't stand the feel of the sludge. She ran her fingers over her dress, desperate to clean them. Problem was, the front of her dress was just as dirty as her hands.

"Are you out here, Jo and Meg?" Jo recognized Amelia's soft voice calling from behind them.

"Yes, we are here, not far from the tracks," Jo answered. "They are directing us to a different train car. Is Sadie with you?"

"Yes," Sadie's voiced chimed in. "Though I think I left part of my--umphf!"

"Oh, watch out for the mud, Sadie!" Meg warned. "Jo just slipped as well."

More like I was pushed! Jo thought, but kept silent.

"That warning would have been a lot more helpful half a second sooner." Sadie groaned. "This mud stinks! I hope all of the dirt in Texas does not smell this way, or I may re-think my engagement."

"Sadie! You shouldn't say that. You gave your word, just like the rest of us," Meg chastised. "You agreed to be a mail order bride. Didn't you sign that contract?"

"Well, it was more of a letter of intent, rather than a contract," Sadie clarified. "And that's all null and void if he failed to mention the ground here smells like manure!"

"It's not the ground here that smells like manure. It's the manure that smells like manure."

At the sound of the deep, masculine voice, Jo's head whipped up. She stopped wiping her fingers on her derriere as her eyes searched the shadows for the voice's source.

The light from a lantern illuminated a tall figure steadily approaching out of the darkness.

The swath of light, streaked with falling rain, cast dancing shadows over the features of the man who carried it, while the rest of his hulking shape was swallowed up in the heavy gloom. His face was chiseled and strong, as if his features were carved from granite. The interplay of light and darkness on his face created startling contrasts, making the strong jaw, defined cheekbones, and deep-set eyes seem even more pronounced.

With the frame of his dark, wavy hair brushing his wide shoulders and blending into the surrounding darkness, his overall impression was striking, almost frightening in its intensity.

And yet, instead of being repelled, Jo was strangely drawn.

"Manure!" Sadie shrieked. "I'm covered in manure?"

"Pete Harding! Boy am I glad to see you!" The engineer rushed past Jo and the other women, sending Jo slightly off balance. Thankfully, she was able to recover quickly before falling into the mud-manure again.

"How did you know we had an accident?" the engineer questioned, completely ignoring the loud twittering of Sadie and some of the other passengers. "We just sent a man to town for help. He couldn't have gotten there already!"

"No, didn't see any man walkin'," the newcomer provided. "Josh and I were checking on the cattle. With the heavy rains we been having, the river that runs through our property has swelled. We were shoring up the fence to make sure the cattle were not gettin' too close to the water. We heard quite the commotion. Sounded like the train came off the rails."

"Oh, it most certainly did!" said the conductor, abandoning his duty of directing passengers to join the conversation. "We definitely hit something."

"Smells like you hit a ranch-full of manure."

"Yes, that's exactly the way it appears," the engineer said grimly.

"I thought we were supposed to be moved to another train car," Meg said at Jo's elbow. "Shouldn't we remind the conductor?"

"I'm already soaked," Amelia complained quietly. "And standing out here isn't improving the situation."

"Shh," Jo hushed, wanting to hear the men's discussion.

The sounds of other passengers loudly complaining further complicated her eavesdropping, and Jo didn't think they'd comply with her hushing as willingly as Amelia.

As casually as she could, she moved closer toward the three men.

"Where are you going, Jo?" Sadie asked loudly.

So much for subtlety. Thankfully, Jo didn't have to answer. Amelia rescued her.

"Look," Amelia said, pointing in the direction from which Pete had walked. "Someone else is coming."

Sure enough, another light from a lantern could be seen. "Let's hope it's someone with a big shovel and a wardrobe of spare dresses," Sadie grumbled. "At the rate we're going, our grooms will have time to send for our replacements!"

"Hello, ladies." The man greeted them. "Are you injured?"

"No," Jo answered. She was the oldest of the group, and the self-appointed leader. "Other than a few bumps and bruises we are fine." The piercing pain in her ribs didn't count. After all, it only hurt when she breathed. If she could figure out how to avoid that, she'd not hurt at all!

"That's good. I'm Josh Harding, by the way. I know this is an unfortunate situation, but let me know if I can assist you ladies in whatever you may need."

Harding. Wasn't that the last name the engineer had called the man named Pete? They must be somehow related.

"Train's not goin' anywhere, Josh." Pete called. "Looks like Mountain Goat Bluff gave out. Guess we found out where George was moving all of the livery's manure. All this rain we been havin' caused a mudslide—well, more like a manure slide. It might take weeks to clear the tracks."

"George put all of the town's manure on top of a cliff?" The man named Josh shook his head, trudging over to where the other men stood. "What was he thinking?"

"I don't know that anyone has accused George of

thinkin'." Pete mused. "But if I had a guess, he probably thought the higher it was, the less likely it would stink."

"What do we do now?" the conductor asked worriedly, gesturing to all of the grumbling passengers comprising their audience.

"How many passengers were on board?" Josh asked.

"Not too many," the engineer replied. "'Bout fifteen. We were headed to Perdition, and this time of night, we're mostly hauling freight."

Josh turned to the conductor. "Any injuries?"

"An older man may have broken his arm, but other than that, doesn't look like it."

"Praise the Lord for that. This could have been much worse." Josh held his lantern higher as he addressed the miserable passengers who were gathered outside the train in the downpour, waiting expectantly for instructions. "I already sent one of my ranch hands to Last Chance on a horse, so more help should be arriving soon. We have a wagon that we can use to help ferry you all into town. But I'm afraid there is not going to be enough room at the hotel for all of you. I have a ranch not far from here. Some of you are welcome to stay there until the tracks are cleared. My wife and I would be happy to have you."

"I can't afford to stay in a hotel," Amelia said quietly in Jo's ear.

"Me either." Sadie echoed.

"Maybe the railroad will pick up the tab," Meg began.

"Maybe they won't!" Sadie shot back. "And even if they pay for the room, I'll still need to eat!"

"Quiet, please!" Jo said, hushing them and stepping forward quickly to address Josh. "Sir, if it would be alright, my friends and I would like to take you up on your kind offer. We are mail-order brides on our way to Perdition. Would it be possible for us to stay at your ranch instead of the hotel?"

She felt Pete's eyes on her, and noticed a strange and pointed dislike emanating from his gaze. Why should he dislike her? Josh had mentioned his wife. Surely it would be right and proper for them to stay there.

"Of course, ma'am," Josh replied quickly. "I'll bring the wagon around."

"Josh, a word, please." Pete's voice was gruff.

"Just a moment, ladies." Josh and Pete walked off a few paces.

"Thank you, Jo," Amelia said.

"Yes, thank you," Sadie echoed. "But what do you think Mr. Goodlookin's problem is?"

"Sadie—," Meg began.

Jo ignored the other women and strained her ears, once again trying to hear what Pete was saying. But the only words she would make out were, "a bunch of hens don't belong on my ranch."

"Wait, did he just call us a bunch of hens?" Jo asked incredulously.

"I don't know," Amelia said doubtfully. "He could have. I can't hear."

"He did!" Jo felt her blood pressure rise as she stomped through the mud to confront the big cowboy.

"Jo, no!" Amelia begged. "We have to stay at his ranch!"

But Jo was wet, she was in pain, and she was definitely not in the mood to be insulted by an inconsiderate cowboy.

Jo came to a stop in front of the duo. "Did you just call us a bunch of hens?" Though her tone was polite, even sweet, she put her hands on her hips, sending the message that, though she was a demure woman, she was not to be trifled with. "I don't appreciate being likened to poultry."

Pete crossed his arms in front of him and shifted his weight to his back foot. Slowly his eyes started at her boots and moved upward.

Jo clenched her fists. She would not squirm and be self-conscious of his scrutiny. It was hard though. She was covered from head to foot in manure.

"I'm sorry, Miss—" the man named Josh started.

"Jo Franklin," Jo said dismissively. Her brown eyes remained locked on the dark shadows where she knew Pete's eyes must reside.

Finally, Pete spoke. "What kind of name is Jo for a woman? Did your parents want a boy and get you instead, or is it short for something else?"

Jo's anger boiled.

"I don't see how my name is any business of yours, sir," Jo said through clenched teeth.

"Oh, it's short for Josephine," Meg's voice volunteered. "I saw it on her ticket."

Jo shot her a withering glance over her shoulder, but it was lost on Meg, who simply smiled innocently in return. Clearly Meg thought she was being helpful.

"Well, Josephine, I did not call you or your fellow womenfolk hens. I wish I did, because it actually seems to be a fittin' comparison the way you are all clucking about, but alas I cannot claim credit. That metaphor is entirely your own."

"I heard you say that those 'hens do not belong on a ranch.'"

"Well, you need to work on your eavesdroppin'. You heard

wrong."

Jo said nothing, grinding her teeth to prevent herself from lashing back. She was a lady. This man was a ruffian. She would not lower herself.

The man seemed to sense her struggle. He quirked one eyebrow, just waiting for her to respond.

"Miss Franklin," Josh stepped forward, blocking Pete from her view. "You, as well as your fellow brides, are welcome at the Bar H. We have more than enough room for all of you. Again, my wife and I... and Pete, are happy to have you."

"Not likely." Pete made a noise of impatience behind Josh. "I'll go get the wagon." With that, Pete and his lantern left.

Jo's anger faded as she watched the man walk away. She felt oddly bereft. Turning back to Josh, Jo said, "Sir, we do not want to put you out or cause problems."

"You won't. Quite the opposite actually. My wife, Addie, is going to love this," Josh grinned. "I think the day she has been praying for has finally arrived."

Pete quickly brought the wagon, and Josh began assisting the women into the back.

"I apologize, ladies. There are a few blankets back there, but they are likely soaked like everything else. We don't have anything to protect you from the rain, but we'll get you to the ranch as soon as we can."

Pete stood sullenly watching as Josh helped the ladies.

"Exactly how many of you are there?" he suddenly burst out as Josh assisted the third lady into the wagon.

"Just four," Jo replied sweetly.

Josh held his hand out to assist Jo, while Pete stalked off like a rooster whose morning crow had just been interrupted.

Jo almost didn't feel the pain of her ribs protest as she

stepped up into the wagon bed. Instead, she felt a rather perverse pleasure to know that four "hens" would be flocking to Pete Harding's ranch.

Chapter 2

The last raindrops retreated, and the morning sun was just peeking through the bank of clouds on the horizon when the wagon carrying Jo and the other brides lumbered to a stop in front of a large, white ranch house.

The front door opened almost immediately, and a blonde-haired woman with a swollen stomach stepped onto the porch.

"There you are, Josh. I was beginning to worry about you."

"No need to worry, Addie." Josh jumped down easily from one side of the wagon, whereas Pete remained seated on the driver's bench. "I brought you back some company. It seems there was a little trouble with the train headed to Perdition."

"Oh, no! What happened?" The woman waddled to the side of the wagon as quickly as she could. Judging by the roundness of her belly, Jo guessed Josh's wife must be nearing the end of her pregnancy.

"A mudslide—" Josh began.

"Manure-slide, you mean," Pete corrected.

Josh shot Pete a warning look over his shoulder and began helping the bedraggled ladies from the back of the wagon by himself.

"The long and the short of it is, the rain washed manure onto the tracks," Josh explained. "The train hit the pile, causing it to derail. No one was seriously injured, but these ladies need a place to stay until the tracks can be cleared. I offered for them to stay here."

"Of course!" Addie exclaimed. "You must stay here at the Bar H. What an awful set of events. Are you certain that you ladies escaped unscathed?"

Jo remained mute as Meg, Sadie, and Amelia confirmed that they were all fine.

"It must have been a lot of manure to cause the train to derail. Where did it all come from?" Addie reached a hand to help Meg from the wagon.

Even a pregnant woman was helping, whereas Pete just sat there looking out at the corrals, ignoring everyone. Jo silently seethed as Josh explained what he knew about the accident.

Pete must have sensed her anger, because he twisted around to see her glaring daggers at him. Jo didn't like the flicker she saw in his eyes as he slowly climbed out of the wagon. He approached her methodically, a slight smirk gracing his lips.

"Miss Josephine." Pete held out his hand to Jo.

She was now the only woman left in the wagon. Jo's heart beat faster as she stared at his waiting hand, and just for a moment, she forgot her ire. His fingers were long and tanned, with callouses marring the surface. Clearly he was not afraid of a hard day's work.

With the sun rising behind her, Jo was able to see Pete clearly for the first time. This man was unlike any Jo had ever seen before. His features were strong and masculine, deeply tanned from days in the sun. Dark hair hung in waves past his shirt collar. It was longer than Jo typically liked, but on this man, it somehow fit. Sooty eyelashes that would be the envy of any woman, rimmed glacier-blue eyes.

One dark brow rose. "Do I pass inspection?"

Jo lifted her chin and grabbed the side of the wagon with both hands. Her traitorous heart might find this ill-mannered brute attractive, but her head knew better.

She flung one leg over the side of the wagon, deliberately knocking Pete's hand out of the way with her boot as she spun. That slap to Pete's wrist proved to be her downfall. Literally. She should have just climbed out carefully, without the dramatic exit she was intending.

But instead... the momentum carried her too far. Instead of her feet gracefully meeting the ground, she landed with her rump meeting the dirt. Air whooshed from her lungs as pain erupted from her bruised midsection.

Apparently, not all of the soil in Texas is soft, Jo thought wryly, clutching her aching ribs.

"Oh, no! Are you hurt?" Addie rushed to Jo's side.

"Don't bend over, Addie," Pete warned. "If you fall on top of her now, yer liable to squish her flat."

"Thanks for pointing that out," Addie said sarcastically, but she nevertheless straightened. "You could have caught her, Pete. You were standing right there."

"I tried to help her, but Miss Josephine must not have seen

my hand. She fairly clobbered it on her way out."

"Well, don't just stand there now, Pete! Help her up!" Addie exclaimed in exasperation.

"There is no need, Mrs. Harding," Jo said, struggling to her feet and refusing to let the pain show on her face. "I am quite alright."

"See there, Addie," Pete boasted, "nothing bruised but her pride."

Jo was a good Christian woman, but at that moment, she was fairly certain she loathed Pete Harding. She was covered from head to toe in manure, her ribs felt shattered, and this man seemed to relish provoking her.

"Pete," Josh stepped between them. "Why don't you drive the wagon on over to the barn and take care of the horses? Addie and I will see to our guests."

"Fine by me," Pete said, lithely jumping into the driver's seat once again.

As Pete pulled away from the house, Addie turned to the four women.

"I don't think we have been properly introduced yet. I'm Addie Harding. Welcome to the Bar H," turning to Jo she continued. "I think I heard Pete call you Josephine is that correct?"

"Yes, but I prefer Jo," Jo said loudly, hoping that her voice might carry to Pete. If he heard her, he showed no response. His back remained to the group in the front yard as the wagon lumbered toward the other scattered buildings.

"Well, then, Jo it is, and all of you must call me Addie. It's lovely to meet you ladies, despite the circumstances. I hope you will enjoy your time here at the ranch, and I look forward to getting to know each of you. Now all of you must be tired and hungry. I was just starting to make breakfast when you arrived. Hot food should be ready shortly. But first, I think you all would enjoy a nice bath and a fresh change of clothing, am I correct?"

Addie's question was answered with vigorous nods from the four women.

"I'm afraid it might take quite a while to heat the water on the stove for four baths, so we'd best get started." Addie turned to lead them up the path to the house.

"Mrs. Harding—I mean, Addie," Sadie called, speaking for the first time since their arrival at the ranch. "Actually, do you have a creek? I think a mess of this magnitude requires a thorough baptism. Every inch of me is covered in manure. I would hate to track this mess into your clean house."

Addie paused. "Well, yes, but are you certain? The creek is not far from here, just a short walk behind the house. Actually, it's more of a small river than a creek. I know from personal experience that it is plenty deep. But I must warn you, although it's summer, it is certain to be a bit frigid this morning."

"Sadie is right," Jo said, stepping forward. "A creek would be more sufficient considering the level of grime we will be removing. I'm sure the temperature will be fine."

"Well then," Addie said, still looking uncertain. "Josh, would you keep the ranch hands away from the creek while the ladies bathe?"

"Of course. Right now they should be busy tucking into their breakfast. They won't disturb you ladies. I will head on over to the bunkhouse to make sure Hank has the grub ready and let them know the creek is off limits."

"Thank you," Addie said, her shoulders releasing some of their tension. "While you do that, I will gather some supplies and show the ladies to the swimming hole. There should be enough privacy there in the shade from the trees. Once they are comfortable, I will finish up breakfast in the kitchen."

Josh strode to a wooden building that Jo assumed was the bunkhouse, while Addie gathered linens for drying and fresh clothing in the main house. She returned shortly with her arms over-laden with baskets.

"Let us help you!" Jo exclaimed, rushing to ease the pregnant woman's burden. "Amelia, please take this basket. And, Sadie, here is the basket of soap. Thank you so much, Addie. It will be so lovely to be clean. Our luggage was left with the train. Your generosity is an answer to prayer."

"And these dresses!" Meg called in surprise, running a delicate blue silk between her fingers. Jo did a double take as well.

"Are you sure you want us to borrow these?" Jo asked, seeing quality of the fabrics. If Addie Harding's wardrobe was any indication, ranching was quite lucrative these days. "They are quite beautiful! Are you certain you wish us to borrow them? We don't want to damage such expensive garments."

"Oh, please, do not worry!" Addie waved her hand, dismissing Jo's fears. "I haven't been able to wear the dresses for several months as you can see. They could use a good airing out. You ladies would be doing me a favor if you wore them."

Jo highly doubted that, but Addie Harding was proving to be a godsend. With their luggage left with the train, and her traveling dress ruined, Jo was very thankful for the borrowed clothing.

Following a worn path just behind the house, Addie led the way to the river while the other women trailed behind carrying the baskets. The peaceful, trickling sound of water could be heard before the trees parted enough to see the sunlight sparkling off the surface of a narrow river. Jo was truly relieved, because she didn't know if she could stand one more minute in her dress which was now stiff with grime.

Jo wasn't alone in her desire to get clean as quickly as possible. Sadie gave a little whoop once she caught sight of the water. She ran past Addie, dropped the basket she carried on the riverbank, and dove headfirst into the water.

She emerged a few moments later, a smile lighting up her face.

"Come on in!" she called. "The water is not cold at all."

"Somehow I don't trust her opinion," mumbled Amelia. "Didn't she say she grew up in Boston or somewhere cold?"

"What I want to know is how are you managing to tread water with your petticoat on?" Addie asked with a laugh. "I nearly drowned when I was in that river with all of my layers of clothes."

"I'm a strong swimmer," Sadie called. "I had to be with a half dozen brothers, and me being the only girl."

"I'm not much of a swimmer myself," Meg said, quietly twisting her hands uncertainly. "Do you think the water is deep?"

"Only toward the middle. If you stay near the bank, it's shallow enough for you to easily touch," Addie said reassuringly. "Now if you ladies have everything you need, I will waddle back to the house and finish up breakfast so that you will have a hot meal to eat and warm yourselves up."

"We will be fine," Jo said, looking up from where she had been arranging the baskets close to the water's edge so they could be easily reached. "Thank you so much for your generosity. You have been so kind to us."

"Please think nothing of it. Josh and I are happy to help. Enjoy your bath."

As Addie headed back to the house, Amelia stepped behind a tree for privacy. Meg remained where she was, staring at Sadie, who began to unceremoniously remove her shoes and clothing, throwing each item onto the river bank with surprising accuracy.

Apparently, swimming isn't the only sport Sadie excels at, Jo thought wryly. *Perhaps having brothers can come in handy.*

"Are you worried about the water, Meg?" Jo asked quietly. "We will be right next to you. I will make sure you are safe."

"It's not just that," Meg said. "What if someone sees us?"

"There are a lot of trees around this part of the river," Jo assured. "I think you are safe from prying eyes."

"Perhaps, but maybe I can just give myself a bit of a sponge bath?"

Apparently Meg's whispers were not quiet enough, because Sadie yelled, "Meg, if you don't get in this water, I will throw you in. A sponge bath is not going to cut it. You stink."

Jo let out an aggravated breath. "Sadie, be nice."

"I'm just being honest."

"I think Sadie's brothers may have been wolves," Meg said under her breath.

Jo burst out laughing. Underneath Meg's proper exterior, she had a sense of humor after all.

"You may be right," Jo said, trying to tamper her giggles. "How about this? I will stand guard and make sure no one approaches while you bathe. That way, you can relax and get clean."

"Are you sure? When will you bathe?"

"I will take my turn when you are done and fully dressed."

"Thank you so much, Jo!" Meg impulsively hugged her. "I am so glad the bride agency sent us to Texas together. I don't know what I would have done without you."

Unused to displays of affection, Jo meekly patted Meg's back.

"You'd better hurry. It looks like Amelia is already in the river. Just make sure you save me some of that lavender soap."

"Absolutely!" Meg called, hurrying to disrobe.

True to her word, Jo walked a few steps away from her fellow brides, and stood watch while they splashed and laughed in the river, rinsing off the remnants of the manure explosion.

"There, Jo," Meg said, emerging from behind a tree a while later. "Now it's your turn."

"You look beautiful!" Jo exclaimed.

"It's the dress," Meg sighed happily. "Have you ever seen anything like it?"

"Look at mine," Sadie twirled, her borrowed emerald green dress setting off her chestnut curls. "I normally don't care for dresses. I like a pair of trousers myself, but this dress just might convert me to the whole institution."

"It is quite the dress," Jo agreed, admiring the rich folds of the fabric. "And you look quite stunning in it."

Movement from behind Sadie caught Jo's eye as Amelia joined the group. "As do you, Amelia."

"Thank you, Jo," Amelia said quietly, ducking her head. Amelia was the quietest of the women. Consequently, Jo knew the least about her. While Sadie and Meg spoke easily about their backgrounds and where they were from, Amelia seemed to have a knack for avoiding answering questions.

"Wait until you see the dress you get to wear," Sadie exclaimed.

"Oh, yes," Meg jumped in excitedly, picking up a lacy

dress from a basket. "Isn't this the most beautiful shade of blue you have ever seen? It looks just like a robin's egg. I can't wait to see it on you, with your dark hair and porcelain skin."

"At this point, I would be happy to wear a flour sack as long as it was clean," Jo said dryly. She knelt and began unlacing her filthy boots. "You three go on back to the house and help Mrs. Harding with breakfast. I'm sure she could use some assistance. She has been so kind, I don't want to burden her with a lot of extra work."

"Shouldn't one of us stay to stand guard?" Meg asked uncertainly.

"I will be fine," Jo tried to yank off her boot, but it wouldn't budge. She plopped down on the riverbank and gave a huge pull. The boot came off with a loud 'thunk.' "You heard Addie. The ranch hands are eating breakfast, and Josh will keep them away. The trees shade this spot. No one will see me."

"Well, if you are sure..." Meg trailed off, still not looking convinced.

"You heard her, Meg. Jo will be fine," Sadie scooped up her sodden clothes and a couple empty baskets. "Let's go. I'm half-starved."

By the time Jo had her boots and stockings removed, the three women were headed back to the house, laden with their things. Even though she was certain that she was alone, Jo hid in the thick foliage that lined the riverbank as she hastily removed her dress and undergarments. Feeling a little foolish after her assurances to the other women, Jo raced into the river and submerged herself in the water.

The water was cool, but Jo found it refreshing. The sun was already starting to heat the morning air, and since she grew up in Maine, Jo was used to frigid water. She had gone ice skating in the winter, and dipped her toes in the chilly waters of the Atlantic Ocean in summer. She could handle a little cold water.

With her long dark hair waving around her, Jo floated on her back, gazing up at the shafts of sunlight that filtered through the trees. She quickly became lost in her memories, thinking of her childhood and the recent events that had led her to this moment. It had been a long journey, in more ways than one, from Maine to Texas.

Jo took several deep breaths. She closed her eyes and savored the stillness and peace of the river. The sounds of the water lapping at the shore, the sweet chatter of birds chirping to each other in the trees above her, the rustling of the bushes to her right as someone passed through them...

Jo's eyes and mouth flew open in surprise. Her arms and legs propelled her toward the shore and the deepest shadows of the bank before her brain even caught up with what was happening.

Problem was, she was on one side of the river, and her clothes were on the opposite side... along with Pete Harding, who just emerged from the brush, fishing pole in hand.

 **Chapter 3**

Jo dipped further into the water until she was sure she resembled an alligator with only her nose, eyes, and top of her head exposed above the water. Hopefully her dark hair blended into the shadows, providing her with some sort of camouflage. Although the porcelain skin that Meg had just complimented her about was not doing her any favors right now. The blinding white against the murky hues of the water would be a dead-giveaway to her location.

Jo felt panic circling around her. She was afraid to even breathe, knowing that the smallest movement would create a ripple that would be easily heard in the quiet morning.

What should she to do? She was trapped in a creek with not a thread of clothing. And a whistling fisherman lay in wait with eyes ready to make his catch.

Jo watched as Pete paused at the edge of the river. Glancing at the sun and then the flowing water, he walked a few paces upstream before settling on a spot. He dug a small container out of his back pocket, opened it and placed what looked like a wiggling worm on the end of his hook.

Without a single glance in her direction, Pete expertly cast his line into the water.

A few moments passed. Jo held her breath, waiting for him to notice her, but he didn't. He just stood there, quietly gazing at the water, seemingly lost in his thoughts.

Should she creep to the bank and make a run for it? But the mere thought sent a wave of shivering panic racing through her. The basket with her clothing sat on the other side of Pete. She'd never make it without being fully visible in all her glory.

Her only option was to wait it out. He would eventually leave, right?

Jo barely caught a sob before it escaped. She had witnessed first hand that Pete Harding was stubborn. She seriously doubted he would leave without a creel full of fish.

What if Pete was a horrible fisherman? She could be stuck without her clothes, cowering in this cold river for hours! She could die from hypothermia!

Jo's dismay faded to anger as the minutes ticked away and she watched Pete continue to slowly reel in his line, oblivious to her dilemma. What was *he* doing here? Of all of the people on this ranch to stumble to the river and begin fishing while she was bathing! It had to be the man that Jo couldn't stand, but also couldn't seem to get away from. Had he come here on purpose?

Jo's anger almost outweighed the embarrassment she felt over her predicament. She so wished she could douse him with a swift kick of her feet in the water!

As the minutes stretched, Jo lost track of their exact

number. Her teeth began chattering. She wrapped her arms around herself, trying to still the shudders. Even with the numbing cold of the water, her ribs ached from the beating they took last night.

She didn't know how much more she could take before she swallowed her pride and revealed herself. Literally.

Dear, Lord, please help me get out of this river with my dignity in tact! She prayed desperately.

Pete continued to methodically cast his line into the water, and ever so slowly, reel it back in.

Well-intentioned heavenly petitions aside, Jo had never hated fishing more.

She shifted her feet in the water. Something tickled her hair.

Oh, no! Was it a bug? Or a bee?

She reached up and bat at her hair, trying to get the offending intruder out, but the tugging just got stronger. Had something larger tangled in her long hair. Had her hair successfully caught a fish where Pete's fancy pole had failed?

Or worse... what if there were snakes in this river?

The more it tugged, the more Jo panicked. Despite her resolve, she began thrashing, trying to get away from the bug/bee/fish/snake.

But the tugging near her scalp only became stronger and more painful as she felt the sharp piercing, worse than a bee sting.

Ouch! What is happening? Jo thought, fully giving up on any attempt to be still.

Her hands whipped above her head, trying to dislodge her attacker, while her feet kicked through the water to get away.

Finally, Jo's hand brushed a thin string.

"She's a big one!" She heard Pete shout excitedly from the shore

Another sharp pull to her hair, and Jo realized she was being dragged to the side of the river by her hair.

"Stop!" Jo screamed, grabbing frantically at what was now a hopeless rat's nest of fishing line tangled in her hair. "Don't reel me in! Your hook is caught in my hair!"

Startled, Pete dropped his pole in the water. Recovering quickly, he snatched at his pole before it was swept away.

"What are you doing?" Pete yelled.

"What does it look like I'm doing?" Jo spat. "Actually, don't look! Turn around right now!"

"What? Why—" Pete's questions died on his lips. Jo saw his eyes widen as realization dawned across his face. He spun away, tangling himself in his own line in his haste.

Serves him right, Jo thought angrily as she frantically ripped at the hook and line in her hair. *I shouldn't be the only one tangled up in this mess.*

"Josephine," Pete called. Jo glanced up from her hook removal task to make sure his back was still turned. It was. And he was free from the line already. "Why exactly are you swimming naked in the river?"

Jo gritted her teeth. "I'm not swimming! I'm bathing!"

"Fine then. Why are you *bathing* in the river when there is a perfectly good tub in the house? I know, because I bought it. Cost a pretty penny too."

"Well, Peter," Jo said sarcastically. If he was going to call her by her full name, she would return the favor. "There are four women and one tub. We were filthy, in case it passed your notice. We didn't want to track manure into Addie's house, and it would have taken all day to heat up water for four baths."

"So you decided it would be a good idea to bathe in the river and not warn people to stay away?"

"I did tell people!" Jo spat. "Well, Josh did. Or he was supposed to. He said he was going to go to the bunkhouse and tell the ranch hands to stay away while we were bathing. Apparently he did a horrible job of it!"

Jo thrashed in the water, trying desperately to untangle herself. It was no use. The line seemed to multiply by the second, and the hook was embedded deep into her hair, occasionally viciously biting into her scalp. She had new sympathy for a fly stuck in a spider's web.

"Don't you go blaming Josh. I wasn't at the bunkhouse."

"Why not? Didn't you want breakfast?"

"I did. I was just about to catch my breakfast, but it appears I caught myself a mermaid instead." Pete glanced over his shoulder. "Or more likely a wildcat."

"Turn around!" Jo yelled.

He complied. "Yep. Definitely a wildcat."

Pete remained silent while Jo pecked at her hair, trying to remove the hook. Each time she thought she was making progress, the clump of hair would worsen. Was she going to have to cut her hair to get the hook out? A sob rose in her throat. Jo wasn't vain, but she would be lying if she said she didn't care about her appearance. She was getting older, in her early thirties, and her hair was still one of her finest features. It was thick and shiny, a sheaf of ebony silk that reached her waist. She didn't want to cut it.

"Stop strugglin' with the hook," Pete ordered. "You're only makin' it worse."

"Don't look!"

"I'm not. I don't need to see you to know that you are making a nice big rat's nest of your hair. I can hear you splashing around like a pig in the mud."

"First, you called me a hen, then a wildcat, and now I'm a pig?" A second sob escaped. This one louder.

"I didn't call you a pig, I said you were splashing like one. Now calm down," Pete spoke slowly and softly. "I can get the hook out."

"But you can't help me! I don't have any clothes on!" All thought to decorum was gone. Jo was wailing now.

"Where is your towel?"

"On the shore to your right," Jo hiccupped. "By that big tree."

"This is what we are goin' to do. I will cut the line on my pole. Once I do that, you can swim on over to the bank and get covered up. Once you are presentable, I will walk on over and help you get the hook out of yer hair."

Jo thought for a moment. His plan could work. She definitely needed help. After all, she didn't have eyes in the back of her head. "Do you promise not to peek?"

"You have my word as a southern gentleman."

"Should have known you were from the South," Jo muttered.

"And I have no doubt you are from the North."

"Of course!" Jo lifted her chin though he couldn't see her. "And proud of it!"

"Then, proud Yankee woman, get out of that there river so I can get my fish hook out of your hair and be on my way. You've cost me my breakfast, my lucky hook, and now my perfectly fine fishing line as well."

Jo felt the release of tension as soon as Pete cut his line.

She watched suspiciously as he walked several yards away to where a clump of trees obscured his view. Through the branches, Jo could still see that his back was turned and his head bent low, as if he were working on the fishing line he'd just cut.

Reasonably certain that she was safe for the moment, Jo hurriedly swam to the side of the creek, waiting until the water was less than a foot deep before she jumped out and splashed to Addie's basket of supplies.

She snatched a towel and wrapped it around her shivering body. Unfortunately, it was an old linen towel that had seen better days, and it provided very little cover. With dismay, Jo looked down and saw the inept towel was the equivalent of a thin, wet napkin plastered against her body.

Like Eve suddenly realizing the extent of her own exposure, she frantically looked around for anything that would offer additional protection. Her eyes scrambled over the foliage, and fortunately she didn't need to sew leaves together. Instead, her gaze lit on the blanket nestled under the basket. It was an old quilt, such as used for picnics, but Jo didn't care about the quality or the purpose. She snatched it up and wrapped it around herself.

Feeling slightly better, she quickly found the clean undergarments Addie had packed. Every movement seemed to cause the hook to painfully dig into her scalp, causing her eyes to water. But, even if it caused serious damage, there was no way she would let Pete touch the hook until every last inch of her was properly covered.

With some very awkward maneuvers that stole her breath with rib pain, she was able to put on the chemise and bloomers without abandoning her blanket cape. Wasting no time, she slipped into the frothy lace dress the girls had talked about. It was actually a blue dress with white lace overlay, and way too exquisite for life on the ranch. Judging by this and the dresses the other girls had been wearing, Jo thought Addie might have an interesting history. Why would an upper-class young woman choose to be a rancher's wife?

Jo's curiosity vanished when she suddenly realized a major problem. The dress's tiny buttons were in the back, where she had no hope of reaching to secure them. A wealthy young woman modeling this type of dress would likely have a lady's maid to help fasten buttons. Jo had no one, except Pete, and there was no way she would ever ask him to fasten her buttons!

Quickly realizing the hopelessness of trying to secure the back herself, she gave up on the open back and wrapped the old quilt securely around her shoulders. Taking a deep breath, she called, "I'm ready!"

The faster Pete removed the hook, the sooner she could escape the creek, Pete, and the awful embarrassment surrounding both.

Pete's footsteps crashing through the brush marked his not-so-subtle approach.

Jo kept her gaze toward the creek, refusing to look at the man. She held the blanket tight around her, with her shivers the only movement in her stiff posture.

"Sit," Pete ordered gruffly.

Jo carefully lowered herself to the ground, making sure every spot of skin was covered, except for her head sticking out the top.

Out of the corner of her eye, Jo caught movement and turned to see the soaring arc of fishing line land with a plop into the water.

Pete then shoved the pole into Jo's hands. "If I'm going to get that hook out, you're going to watch my pole. Thankfully, I have enough line to make another attempt at breakfast."

"I don't think I'm really qualified—"

"All you have to do is hold the pole. If you feel a tug, hand it to me."

Jo bit her lip and resigned herself to holding the pole stiffly as she braced it against the blanket. She had not been fishing since she was a child. Though those memories of fishing with her grandparents were still some of the fondest of her entire life, she still didn't feel that qualified her to fish. But, if not arguing with Pete meant that he would remove the hook faster, then she was willing to hold his fishing pole.

Though she'd been expecting it, she had to keep herself from jumping at the touch of his hands on her hair. With amazingly gentle movements, she felt his big hands carefully sort through her hair and the fishing line, extracting strands away from the hook.

It was a strange sensation to have those calloused, work-roughened fingers work almost tenderly, trying not to cause her unnecessary pain. She realized that he could have simply offered to cut the hook away, but that would have sacrificed a good chunk of her hair in the process. So instead, the minutes ticked away as he carefully untangled each strand and removed it from danger.

There was something relaxing about the silence and the way the shadows of the current danced in the light. Jo found her muscles relaxing to the music of the lulling trickle of the river. Having those big hands immersed in her hair sent goose bumps through her body, but it was also strangely soothing.

If she used just a little imagination, she could almost feel what it would be like for those gentle movements to be the caressing ministrations of a man she couldn't help but be attracted to.

Startled at the direction of her thoughts, Jo snapped out of her hypnosis and blurted the first thing that popped into her mind. "How long do you think it will take to clear the tracks? My fiancé is waiting for me in Perdition. I don't want to worry him."

Hopefully, the mere mention of her fiancé would vanquish any thoughts of romance, on the off-chance that Pete felt even a fraction of the strange attraction that was victimizing her.

But, if she was being honest, she would have to admit that the reminder was really more for herself.

"I think it will take several weeks to fully clear that mess," Pete replied easily. "But I imagine the train will make other arrangements to get you to your destination before that or just clear the tracks enough for the train to pass. We certainly wouldn't want to worry a man you've never met."

Jo bristled. "We've corresponded."

Technically, "corresponded" might be stretching the truth a little bit. She had received a letter from him, and written a letter back, but none of that was Pete's business!

"So I'm right. You've never met this man you've agreed to marry," Pete persisted. "Is there a shortage of men in the North where you ladies are from?"

"No!" Jo denied, aghast. "Besides, we are not all from the same place, and we all had our different reasons for choosing to be mail order brides."

She felt, rather than saw, Pete shake his head. "Fool women. I would think it would be less risky to marry a man you knew, rather than one you didn't. What if your intended has a wooden leg, one eye, and spends his days drunk?"

Jo's mouth fell open, appalled at the idea. "We went through an agency!" she protested. "All of the men are pre-qualified as respectable, God-fearing men. I wouldn't have agreed otherwise!"

Pete snorted. "And how does the agency do it? Are the men rounded up like cattle, hosed off for sale, and then matched with a fine heifer? What does pre-qualified mean? Are they weighed, measured, and approved for auction to make sure they aren't as ugly as my mule?"

If Pete hadn't been holding onto her hair, she would have turned on him and lectured in all her fury.

"I can't speak for the other women," she bit out. "They all have their own reasons for being mail order brides. I can only speak for myself. And my reasons, and my life, are none of your concern! For your peace of mind, however, I will inform you that the man I am to marry is a respectable widower with his own ranch, which is a vast departure from your wooden-legged drunk who resembles a mule!"

At that exact moment, Jo felt a strong jerk on the pole in her hands.

"Oh!" Jo gasped, instinctively jerking the pole upward.

Jo had just caught Pete's breakfast.

Chapter 4

"Reel it in! Reel it in!" Pete ordered, springing to his feet.

Jo jumped up with him. Looking down, she saw a fancy, new reel affixed to the pole. Shocked as she was, she obeyed, turning the reel to bring the line in, while fighting against the weight tugging on the other end.

But the river wasn't that wide. How much did she have to reel, and how fast?

She lowered the pole to try to get a better grip against its jerking movements.

"Keep the tip up!" Pete shrieked. "He'll get away!"

Panicked, Jo jerked the tip back up hard and fast. At the force of the movement, the fish shot out of the water to land smack in Pete's face.

Pete clawed at his face, or rather the fish, trying to capture the slippery creature as it slid toward the ground. His hands fluttered haphazardly, grabbing at the fish even as he tried to retreat from its onslaught.

The slippery thing hit both his hands, then his chest. Finally, it slid down the length of him all the way to the dirt.

At the sight of the flopping fish at her feet, Jo shrieked and dropped the pole. Her feet danced on tiptoes as she tried to escape the fish. In her haste, she forgot to secure her blanket, which ended up on the ground, tangling around her tiptoeing feet until she tripped completely and landed with her backside nestled in its folds.

Pete finally nabbed the fish right before it made a final flop into the water. Triumphantly, he held it up high. Instead of anger at Jo's awkward landing of the fish, a grin stretched across his face.

"Isn't he a beauty?" he asked, holding all sixteen inches of fish up for inspection.

"I thought you said I just had to hold the pole!" Jo accused from her seated throne on the blanket.

"I thought you had it handled!" Pete shot back, quickly stringing the fish up and placing it back in the water with a rock to hold the stringer secure. "I could tell it was a big 'un, and didn't want to risk it getting away when we switched the pole. Had I known you were going to beat me with the thing..."

"You told me to keep the tip up!" Jo defended, stubbornly crossing her arms in front of her.

"I'm sorry! I didn't realize you were such an overly-obedient creature. But the fact that you slung a fish in my face fully convinces me that I have misjudged your willingness to cooperate with my wishes." Pete reached up and stroked his chin. "Now that I think about it, a cooperative Josephine Franklin could come in very handy."

"Are you going to finish removing this hook or not?" Jo seethed. The faster she could get away from this brute, the better!

"Of course," Pete replied, setting his pole down beside Jo and returning to his position behind her. "I was almost done. As long as you didn't do more damage with your antics, I should have my hook back shortly."

Jo gritted her teeth, but didn't reply. If he valued the welfare of his hook above her, then there wasn't anything more to say.

However, at the touch of his hands at her back, electricity coursed through her like streaks of icy lightning. Pete gathered her long, dark hair together and placed it gently over her shoulder. He then began fastening the tiny bead buttons down the back of her dress.

With everything that had happened the past few minutes, Jo hadn't realized she'd been sitting there with her back exposed to her undergarments. Now, without a single word, snide or otherwise, Pete carefully matched each bead with its hole.

Jo swallowed, remaining silent as embarrassment coursed through her. She had to remind herself to be thankful for two things. One, that Pete couldn't see her pink-tinged face; and two, that the undergarments Addie had provided were thick and modest. While she was confident that she hadn't been indecently exposed, the embarrassment of having Pete fasten her up over anything labeled an "undergarment" was embarrassing enough.

With Pete's silence continuing as he worked, Jo finally had to release the breath she held. To her surprise, he actually wasn't going to say a word about her buttons and the state of her undress! Unfortunately, that was curious in and of itself. Why did Pete seem to take such joy in aggravating her, and yet when something happened when he could rightfully ridicule her unmercifully, he remained silent, tenderly helping her keep her dignity?

Tickling sensations followed Pete's movements down her back, and Jo felt a sense of pleasure that she'd never recalled feeling before. She'd never had a man touch her in such a personal way.

Was it normal to feel such chills radiating from a simple touch?

Was it wrong to wish there were about five hundred buttons for him to fasten?

Much too soon, Pete finished with the buttons and moved back to her hair.

Once again, Jo had to fight the urge to lean into his touch and fully enjoy the sensation of his hands lightly fingering through her tresses. She eventually shut her eyes, trying to pray and focus on the man she was to marry and not the man doing strange things to her heart.

She wondered what Oscar Pruitt looked like. Would her fiancé be handsome, or more mule-ish like Pete had suggested? She wished a picture had been included with the letter presented her by the agency. In spite of herself, Pete's words had given her cause to worry. What if Oscar Pruitt did have a wooden leg?

Jo mentally shook herself. She was a practical woman, not given to flights of fancy, which was exactly why she had agreed to be a mail order bride. It had been sensible, given her rather dire circumstances.

Now she attempted to calm herself, deliberately trying to picture her intended as an attractive man. Tall, strong, dark hair, rugged, with deep-set eyes the color of a deep turquoise-blue glacier.

"All done," said a quiet voice that matched the face in Jo's head.

Jo opened her eyes and looked down to see a fishing hook lying in Pete's hand, as if he was presenting it to her. Jo automatically picked it up with delicate fingers, inspecting it while wondering how something so small could cause so much trouble.

However, instead of standing and moving away with the completion of his task, Pete hesitated. Reaching over to Addie's basket, he pulled something out. "If you don't mind, I made a bit of a mess of your hair."

Then he began gently pulling a brush through the long length of Jo's hair.

And it was almost Jo's undoing. She practically melted to the blanket. A longing filled her heart and tears rimmed her eyes. Never had she felt so cared for. The aggravating brute of a man was tenderly brushing her hair. And she let him.

Once again closing her eyes, she was helpless to stop her body from leaning into his ministrations. Gradually, the slow movements of the brush stilled and Pete's hands moved to her shoulders.

"I feel like I should explain..." Pete said softly, his voice cracking. "I'm a rough man. Things don't always, or usually, come out right when I speak. I didn't mean to offend you earlier when speaking of your fiancé. I guess I'm just a bit mystified why a woman who... isn't as ugly-as-my-mule would choose to marry a man she'd never set eyes on. And those widowers... Around here, if a man is a widower, there might be at least a decent chance he had part in making himself that way. Men don't always treat their women well. I'd hate to see that happen to you."

Jo's heart beat fast, though it seemed to forget to beat at all when she thought about Pete's words saying she wasn't as ugly as a mule. Why should that thrill her so much?

Part of her longed to hold onto a little of the offense, just to distance herself from him, but his thoughtful concern was enough to earn any forgiveness needed. Though her mouth felt dry and she longed to turn into his arms and look him in the eyes, she remained seated forward. She knew that if she gave into her desires, Pete would be able to clearly read the emotions flooding her eyes.

Instead, she replied stiffly, struggling to keep her tone devoid of the tenderness it wanted to convey. "I appreciate your concern. And I have to admit, I am not used to having anyone concerned over my welfare, so I know I am not always the most gracious myself. However, let me assure you that I am a godly woman. I've made my decision with much prayer, and I believe it was a wise decision, given my particular circumstance. I went through an agency so as to be the safest and wisest possible. They have done the necessary screenings, and I am confident both, that I am in God's will, and that He will place me in my husband's good hands."

Her speech made, Jo stood up swiftly, trying to ignore the bereft feeling of losing the warmth of Pete's hands on her shoulders. All business now, she swept the twigs and dirt from her dress and began to gather the brush and other items to return to Addie's basket.

"Thank you for your assistance, Mr. Harding," Jo said formally.

Pete watched her movements in silence. Finally, he spoke, "Seems rather silly not to call each other by our given names; don't you think, Josephine? Calling you Miss Franklin seems rather awkward considering I've seen you as the good Lord made you."

Jo whirled around in shock. She felt heat rise from her neck into her face, but didn't know whether it was caused more by embarrassment or anger. Her first instinct was that the rough man had just misspoken, but by the glint of orneriness in his eyes, Jo knew he realized exactly what he'd said.

Swift, fierce fury shot through her. It was anger at his words, but perhaps even more anger at Pete toying with her. One minute he was aggravating her; the next minute making her long for him in a very unfamiliar way; and then the next, he was back to insulting.

Before she fully realized what she was doing, she picked up Pete's fishing pole from where it lay at her feet. Then, with all her might, she threw it into the creek.

Pete let out a strangled gasp, and clothes and all, he leapt into the creek to rescue his pole.

With hands on her hips, Jo stood on the bank and called to him, "*Mr. Harding*, I'm fairly certain you did not see me 'as the good Lord made me.' I am equally certain that your mother did not birth you with a fishing pole in your hand. So, as far as I'm concerned, you can leave this creek without your pole, just as the good Lord made you!"

Not sparing a single backward glance, Jo picked up the basket and blanket and marched away from the creek, not even noticing she still held Pete's lucky fishing hook clenched carefully in her hand.

Chapter 5

"I am so sorry to keep everyone waiting," Jo said as she rushed into the dining room of the ranch house.

It was evening, and Jo had acquiesced to Addie's assertions that she should rest after her harrowing ordeal the night before. Apparently, Jo was more tired than she thought, and in more pain than she cared to admit. She had slept the entire afternoon, awaking to long shadows on her guest bedroom walls.

"You didn't keep us at all. Your timing is perfect. We were just sitting down," Addie assured her. "Why don't you take the place next to Meg?"

Jo hurried to the empty chair. She slid into her seat only to look up into a pair of blue eyes that she had hoped she would never see again. Well, that may not be entirely honest, but she did wish that Pete might be absent from the dinner table as he had been at breakfast.

Thoughts of Pete's "breakfast" warmed Jo's cheeks.

Pete's mouth curved ever so slightly at the corners as if he too was remembering their last meeting. Of all of the places at this large table, why did she end up across from him? It seemed like every time she turned around, he was directly in her path.

Determined to ignore him and his blue eyes, Jo pretended to be absorbed in unfolding her napkin and re-arranging her silverware around her plate.

"Josh, would you pray over the food, please?" Addie asked.

"Of course," Josh bowed his head. "Dear Lord, thank you for this food and for your provisions. Thank you for new friends, and for keeping them safe and free from injury in the train accident. Please bless the food and the hands that prepared it. Amen."

Jo felt a tiny prickle of guilt that she had not been honest about her injury. She hoped that resting that afternoon would heal her sore ribs, but they were more tender and painful now than they were this morning.

"I'm afraid we are rather informal here," Addie said, holding up a steaming bowl of corn. "It's usually just Josh, Pete, and me, so we just pass the dishes."

"This is the way I like it," Sadie smiled, accepting the dish. "Feels like home."

"The food looks wonderful, Addie," Jo marveled. "I didn't intend to sleep the day away. I am sorry that I failed to help you in the kitchen once again."

"No need to apologize! You were overly tired. Meg, Sadie, and Amelia were plenty of help. I'm glad you were able to rest. You looked a little flushed after your bath in the river. I hope it wasn't too cold."

"It was fine," Jo rushed to change the subject, refusing to glance at Pete. "I'm relieved to hear that you had help, but I insist on washing the dishes after dinner."

"You don't have to do it by yourself," Addie said. "I'm sure Pete can help you as well."

Pete again! "That's not necessary. I'm sure he's worked a long day."

"Nope. Just been fishin'."

Jo shot Pete a warning glare.

"Yes, Pete took the day off it seems," Josh joked good-naturedly as he loaded his plate full of food. "But since he caught us dinner, I will let it go."

"Well, Mr. Harding, you must be quite the fisherman." Sadie gestured to the plate of fried trout that was making its way around the table. "There must be a dozen trout here! They are all good sized, and that one on Josh's plate must be a good seventeen inches!"

"Yep. And that's not the biggest fish I caught today." Pete's eyes twinkled as he gazed at Jo.

"Really!" Sadie exclaimed. "What happened to that one? I don't see it. Was it a trout?"

"Nope. It was the meanest catfish I've ever done met."

"A catfish?" Meg asked incredulously, her eyes wide in alarm. "Do they bite?"

"No, silly," Sadie answered.

"I didn't think there were catfish in our river," Addie mused.

"There aren't," Josh said dryly, eying his uncle suspiciously.

Oh, no, thought Jo. *Where is Pete headed with this? Is he going to tell everyone that I was his catfish?*

Jo glared daggers at Pete, but he just smiled wider.

"Well, I found one. Maybe it swam down from up north. It was definitely a mean sucker. A Yankee fish to be sure."

"You're one to talk about Yankees, Pete," Josh said around a mouthful of fish. "You served in the Northern army. You might as well be called a Yankee too."

Jo looked up in surprise. "You didn't serve in the Confederate army? But you're from the South."

"That I am. Southern born and bred. But let's not change the subject. We were talking about fishing."

"What did your family think about you serving in the Union?" Jo asked refusing to be deterred.

"That's a story for another day." Pete met Jo's eyes, the teasing light vanishing for just a moment. Jo's breath caught and her heart began to hammer. With her gaze locked with Pete's, the other people at the table faded from view until it seemed as if she and Pete were alone in the room.

Clearing his throat, Pete broke the connection.

Jo blushed as she realized what the others might think of their little staring contest.

"Let's see, where was I?" Pete leaned back in his chair, his meal seemingly forgotten. "Oh, yes, hooking the catfish. It was quite the surprise, let me tell you, when my hook got set in that fish and I started to reel it in. Boy, did it put up a fight. Thrashing about. It would have liked to rip my pole clean out of my hands. Come to think of it, it did make off with my lucky fish hook."

"Whatever will you do?" Jo asked innocently. "I trust you can manage without it?"

"No, 'fraid I can't. But don't worry, I got a good look at

that fish before it swam off." Pete's eyes twinkled dangerously.

Jo's cheeks burst into flame.

How dare he!

But Pete wasn't finished. "I'm sure I will see it again someday. Maybe get my hook back too."

"No, sir, you will not," Jo announced with conviction.

A shocked silence accompanied Jo's statement. All eyes were on her.

Jo grappled for something to say that wouldn't make her sound crazier than she already did. "Uh, I mean..."

Words evaded her. What had she done? Why hadn't she just kept her mouth shut! No, instead she continued to take the bait whenever Pete dangled it in front of her!

Jo winced. Now she was thinking of herself as a fish! What had this man done to her? "What I mean is... I... um..."

"Why, it seems Josephine doubts my capabilities," Pete quipped.

But he was the only person at the table smiling, and if Jo didn't want to strangle him, she might allow herself a moment to admire how white and even his teeth were, or how his smile lit up his eyes and made them seem to glow with blue fire.

Angry with herself, Jo snapped, "No, that is not it."

Oh, just be quiet! Jo's inner voice chastised. But while her inner voice reasoned that the best way out of the potentially humiliating conversation was to remain silent, she couldn't help herself. She simply couldn't turn off her emotions where Pete was concerned.

"Hmm…" Pete mused thoughtfully. "If Josephine doesn't doubt my abilities, perhaps she is an animal sympathizer. Am I right?"

"Huh?" Sadie asked, looking as dumbfounded as Jo.

Pete wiggled his eyebrows. "She roots for the fish."

Sadie stared at Jo as if she had grown two heads. "Why would she do that?"

"Beats me," Pete said, gazing at Jo with a wide grin on his face.

Jo might have been angry, but she was so relieved that the conversation was drifting away from Pete's morning fishing trip, she almost didn't care that Pete sported a satisfied grin as he leaned back in his chair with his arms crossed and relaxed.

"Pete, I think the term you are looking for is a vegetarian," Addie said.

"A vege-what?" Sadie asked.

"Vegetarians do not eat meat," Addie said calmly. "Jo, are you a vegetarian? I can cook you some other food if you would like."

"Oh, Addie—" Jo began.

But Sadie interrupted, waving her hand dismissively. "I can tell you for sure that Jo is not a vegetablarian, or whatever. She had a whopping pile of bacon this morning at breakfast, and she sure wasn't 'rootin' for the pig.'"

Jo laughed. "You are certainly right, Sadie. I am not a vegetarian. I do eat meat, and, Addie, the fish you cooked is especially delicious. Thank you."

After that, the conversation moved to other subjects, and the spotlight was no longer on Jo. Jo was so relieved she could almost thank Pete for ridiculously suggesting that she was a vegetarian. Despite her anger toward him, she knew he had deliberately come to her rescue.

Which is why she felt the need to thank him a half hour later when they were standing side-by-side at the kitchen sink washing the dinner dishes. The rest of dinner had passed easily and without further embarrassment. When everyone else retired to the parlor with coffee, Jo and Pete set to work on cleaning up.

The kitchen was uncomfortably silent. At least it was for Jo. One quick side glance at Pete revealed that the ever present half-smirk was adorning his handsome face.

Stop it! Jo scolded herself. He was rude. Uncouth. Not the least bit refined. He had teased her unmercifully at the dinner table tonight, and came very close to exposing Jo, this time figuratively rather than literally.

Jo's cheeks warmed at the thought.

But for some strange reason, he had come to her rescue later when she had made the situation worse by striking back at him. Granted, he deserved every bit of her ire, but he could have left her to languish miserably when words evaded her. He might have no sense of social decorum, but Jo felt obligated to express some sort of gratitude.

"Thank you, Mr. Harding," she spoke finally, her throat dry around the words. "Thank you for not telling everyone about the incident at the river this morning, and for supplying words when I found myself at a loss for what to say."

There she had done it.

But unable to resist, she couldn't help adding, "Though you could have refrained from the innuendos and teasing in the first place." Apparently she wasn't as thankful or forgiving as she originally thought.

"You are welcome... Josephine."

Any good will vanished.

"Stop calling me Josephine!" Jo fumed, literally stamping her foot. "I have not given you permission to address me as anything other than Mrs. Franklin!"

"Missus, you say?" The teasing light died in Pete's eyes. "So you've been married before?"

"That is none of your business!" Jo sputtered, splaying soap suds all over her dress. "Honestly, Mr. Harding, I don't know that I've ever met a man so lacking in normal social decorum! And furthermore, just to clarify your earlier accusation as to where my sympathies lie, lately I feel a kinship towards animals as I have not felt before. This could be due to the fact that you have referred to me as a hen, a wildcat, and a fish all in less than twenty-four hours' time!"

"Josephine," Pete replied sternly. "I am a simple man. Like most men around here, I tell things as I see them. If that offends your proper sensibilities, then maybe the problem lies with you. As for me, if a woman behaves like a hen, a wildcat, or a fish, that is not an insult. I like animals. However, I can't guarantee this man you're headed to marry will appreciate such behavior nearly as much as I do."

Jo's mouth opened and closed in shock. How dare he insinuate that she was anything but a proper lady! He was the one being rude!

As if he knew he'd found a weakness, Pete dug a little deeper, "Tell me, do you think your husband knows what kind of wife he purchased at the auction? Does he know you're not a miss, but a missus?"

In a haze of anger, Jo flung her arms down and opened her mouth to tell Pete Harding exactly what she thought of him. But her hand caught the dishwater with such force that it spouted up, right into Pete's smug face.

He sputtered, blinking while gray water slowly dripped down his face.

"Oh!" Jo started, completely shocked. "I'm sor—"

But before she could finish her apology, she was sputtering on dishwater herself, courtesy of Pete's generous splash.

Not bothering to think things through, she retaliated, grabbing a handful of soap suds and tossing them at Pete's dark eyebrows. She may not have intentionally started the fight, but she sure wasn't going to back down now!

Pete grabbed her and swung her around, pinning her hands so he could rain bubbles over her hair. She reached out and snatched the dishtowel with her free hand. Reaching up behind her, she rubbed it in his face, hoping she could wash off that perpetual smirk once and for all.

Sputtering, he let her go.

She swung around just as he lifted the entire tub of dishwater and paused, staring at her.

Jo looked around for a weapon. But the only thing she saw was the pan of grease Addie had used to fry the fish. She grabbed for it, then looked at Pete, daring him to make his move.

"Jo? Pete?" Addie's voice called. "Everything okay in there?"

Frantic, Pete set down the basin of water, and Jo practically flung her pan of grease back on the counter. Both of them turned and stood at attention, with arms straight at their sides and their faces filled with the guilt of naughty children.

Addie peeked her head into the kitchen, but didn't cross the threshold.

"Yes, Addie, we're doing just fine," Jo managed to squeak. "We're just… taking our time."

Pete cleared his throat. "Yes, ma'am. Just like a couple pigs enjoying a roll in their slop."

Addie laughed and turned away, never bothering to actually enter the kitchen. "Well, hurry up. The girls are talking about playing a game, and we could use a couple more players."

Jo and Pete wordlessly turned back to the dishes. Jo handed him a dry towel, and then picked up a bowl and began vigorously scrubbing while trying to brainstorm ways she could sneak up to her room for a dry change of her borrowed clothes.

Finishing the bowl, she rinsed it and handed it to Pete to dry. Her gaze fluttered up to his.

They stared at each other, completely silent, locked in a place where time skipped a beat.

Pete slowly lifted his towel and gently wiped a stray bubble from her cheek.

And she let him.

Chapter 6

Jo obediently raised the parasol, and then glanced back at the house to make sure Addie was watching through the kitchen window. She hadn't wanted to seem ungrateful to her sweet hostess, but she thought this bluish-white bit of lacy fluff on a stick was more than a little ridiculous.

Never would she have dreamed of saying so to Addie, especially when the woman had excitedly presented Jo with a pair of lacy gloves and a parasol that exactly matched her borrowed dress. Jo had no choice but to accept the gift with compliments on how beautiful they were, and then continue on her way to join the other ladies for a walk outside.

As the parasol splayed delicately above her head, she could clearly read Addie's delighted smile through the window. It was obvious that Addie was from an affluent background, and it was equally obvious that it somehow gave the woman joy to see her old things used by her unexpected guests. So, no matter how ridiculous Jo looked touting an elegantly flimsy parasol that was no more effective at blocking the shade than a sieve was at holding water, she would do so with pride, even if it wasn't appreciated by her audience of livestock in their corrals.

With a little wave of her lacy gloved hand, Jo turned from Addie to locate the other ladies. They had a head start on their afternoon walk since Jo had insisted on staying to help Addie finish the lunch dishes, but Jo didn't think they had gone far. Three women shouldn't be too difficult to locate on a ranch.

Jo picked her way through the uneven mud around the closest corral, wishing Addie had permitted her to wear more appropriate footwear for a walk. But since Addie was in heaven with having four women to dress up, nothing but fashionable boots sporting a tiny little heel would be permitted with an elegant dress such as Jo wore.

Jo rounded a large barn. Her ankle twisted on a rock, but she ignored the pain and resolutely trudged ahead to where her friends were lined up along a fence up ahead. She was relieved to see that the ladies were alone. Not that she was expecting they would be joined by Josh, Pete, or any of the other ranch hands, but she was still wary, especially of Pete. That man had a knack for showing up where he wasn't expected. Though Jo took it as an encouraging sign that he had been absent at both breakfast and lunch today, she wouldn't put it past him to show up to aggravate her at a moment's notice.

Jo watched as her friends bobbed up and down in strange patterns, wandering around the front of the fence. With their colorful gowns, they looked dressed for a high society engagement, not for adorning the worn fence at a ranch.

"What are you doing?" Jo asked, drawing near to the elegant baubles.

"Oh, good! You're here!" Sadie exclaimed with eyes bright.

"Aren't these wildflowers pretty? We're picking some for Addie. What do you think? I thought we should focus on the yellow and blue ones, but Amelia liked some white and purple mixed in. And Meg… didn't Meg want some pink?"

"Yes, I believe so," Amelia answered with a shy smile. "Jo, what a beautiful parasol! Isn't it sweet of Addie to spoil us so! I wish I had something more than flowers for her."

Jo looked up at her parasol. She had to admit, it was very pretty the way the sunlight filtered through the elegant blue material with lace overlay. She carefully folded the parasol back up compactly. If she was going to be picking flowers, she didn't want to risk ruining what was obviously an expensive accessory.

The girls were right, Addie would enjoy some flowers for her table. And with the recent rain, there seemed plenty to choose from.

Tucking the parasol under her arm, Jo bent to retrieve a spray of dainty white flowers, trying to ignore the burst of pain across her ribs. She straightened quickly, hoping the others hadn't noticed her wince.

Thankfully, the other two women were still busy making their floral choices.

"Where is Meg?" Jo asked, suddenly realizing they were missing one of their usual foursome.

"Oh, she's around here somewhere," Sadie said offhandedly, bending to retrieve a bunch of delicate yellow flowers at her feet.

Amelia stopped and turned, shielding her eyes to look for their friend. "I think she said she saw some pink flowers somewhere," she said quietly.

Jo followed suit, lifting her hand to block the bright sunlight from her eyes and scanning the entire area.

Her gaze focused on Meg's pink gown, the only color in the open field beyond the fence. She had wandered quite a ways off and was facing the other direction as she bent over, following what Jo supposed was a trail of flowers.

Jo lifted her voice to call for Meg to come back, but catching movement out of the corner of her eye, any sound died before it cleared her throat.

A large, black beast paced back and forth on the side of the field opposite Meg.

Jo knew enough to realize this was not an ordinary cow.

It was a bull.

Her heart leapt into her throat as terror seized her. She longed to call out to Meg and warn her, but what if her call attracted the animal's attention?

Maybe it wasn't dangerous. After all, right now the bull seemed content to pace back and forth.

But Jo knew better. There had to be a reason the bull was alone in the field. Jo was sure the bull had seen Meg, and while he was currently keeping his position, he was watching warily. Any sudden movement from Meg could incite his fury.

"Amelia... Sadie..." Jo croaked, getting the attention of the other two women. "There's a bull in there with Meg."

Amelia gasped.

Sadie straightened from her flower picking. "Well, she should probably get out of there," she said casually. Then cupping her hand over her mouth, she shouted, "Meg, get out of there! There's a bull!"

"No—!" Jo gasped, trying to stop Meg, but it was too late; the damage was already done.

At Sadie's call, Meg straightened and turned around, as if confused.

Jo knew the moment Meg saw the bull. Her body went rigid, and she slowly backed up.

To Meg's credit, she kept her movements small and slow as she tried to make her way back to the fence.

But the bull noticed.

His pacing changed. He switched directions, placing Meg in a direct line between him and the fence. He tossed his head repeatedly. His hoof beat a rhythm pawing at the ground.

Abandoning all caution, Meg panicked, turning to run as fast as she could for the fence.

The bull charged.

"Go get help!" Jo shrieked, watching in horror as the bull gained on Meg.

Amelia and Sadie took off, following her orders, but Jo's focus was entirely on the terror flushing Meg's face.

Please, Lord. Help her! she prayed, her heartbeat rivaling her friend's speed across the uneven field.

Meg wasn't going to make it.

The second Jo realized Meg's fast pace wasn't going to be enough, she reacted. She climbed the fence and swung her leg over. Leaping down, she began running straight for the bull. She grabbed the parasol from under her arm and carried it with her, not even noticing its presence in her tight grip. She stumbled, her feet twisting on her heeled boots, and yet she still kept running.

The bull saw Jo coming. Seeming mildly distracted or confused, his pace slowed, as if trying to decide which one of the women to charge.

Jo reached them right as he was about to overtake Meg. Realizing she had the parasol in her hand, she swung it like a bat and whacked the bull in the nose as he passed.

The bull stopped short, grunting and shaking his head.

"Get out!" Jo yelled at Meg. Holding the lace parasol outstretched like a weapon, she placed her body between the other woman and the bull.

The bull snorted, glaring at Jo.

Jo backed off slowly, but the bull stepped forward, ramming his face toward Jo. Not knowing what else to do, Jo thrust her parasol forward, trying to get him to back off.

But with the bull's own movement, the pointed tip of the parasol thrust right up his nose!

The bull hollered, backing up and thrashing his head.

The tip of the parasol came out. Though it was intact, it would likely never again resemble white.

Jo shot a look behind her. Meg had made it safely over the fence and was hopping up and down, hysterically crying from the safety beyond the corral.

Jo hurriedly back pedaled, calculating her chances of just making a run for it. She didn't want to turn her back on the bull, but she needed to get out.

The bull paused his shaking, as if noticing her attempted escape. Looking directly at him, Jo saw what looked like a red haze film over his eyes. And Jo knew he was mad.

She held the parasol up, determined to shove it up his nose again if necessary.

Her feet spun backward. She was almost there. She reached out behind her, her fingers stretching to grasp the rail of the fence.

She would have made it. Another few steps and the tips of her fingers would have closed around the rail.

If not for Addie's spiked boots...

The heel of Jo's right boot caught in the soft mud. Her

momentum flung her backward, propelling her through the air until she came in for a landing, flat on her backside. The force sent pain searing through her, stealing her breath and seizing any movement.

She couldn't breathe. She couldn't move. And she knew what was coming.

Helplessly, she squinted up to see the bull charging straight at her.

She feebly lifted the parasol, knowing that it wouldn't keep her from being trampled.

Dear, Lord! Jo closed her eyes and braced herself for the impact.

But the sudden shouting and clanging of metal was not what she anticipated.

Her eyes flew wide to see Pete shouting at the bull while beating a metal pan and charging at the beast with the ferociousness of an animal equal in size.

Startled, the bull slowed, looking from Pete to Jo and back again.

Nearing the bull, Pete took the wooden post in his right hand and smacked the bull across the nose.

As if properly chastised, the bull shook his head. Then his horns bowed low in shame, and he fully retreated before Pete's continued chase.

Jo leaned her head back and shut her eyes. *Thank you for Pete.*

She breathed in and out slowly, tears squeezing from the corners of her eyes. She didn't know if the tears were from relief or pain. All she knew was that she couldn't make them stop.

A couple minutes later, she was still debating whether she

could move when she felt someone kneel beside her.

"Where are you hurt, Jo?" asked a gruff voice.

Jo opened her eyes to find Pete looking down at her in concern.

"I'm okay," Jo said, wetting her dry lips. "Maybe you can just help me up."

Pete gently pulled her to her feet, but as soon as she was upright. Pain crushed her ribs and she groaned, her feet collapsing beneath her.

Pete caught her, lifting her easily into his arms. He hurriedly climbed over the fence, managing to keep her tucked close.

"Tell Addie to send one of the ranch hands for the doctor," he ordered roughly as he passed the other women.

Pete grumbled all the way to the house, but Jo's pain was so severe, she had trouble deciphering it.

"Don't know why a fool woman would get in the corral with a bull. Could have been killed."

"She was rescuing me!" Meg's shaky voice answered from where she trotted by Pete's elbow. "I was picking flowers. I didn't know there was a bull. It's all my fault. If Jo dies because of that bull…"

"I'm not going to die," Jo managed breathlessly. "The bull didn't hurt me. I was hurt in the train accident. My ribs…"

"You were injured and you didn't say anything?" Pete bit out.

Jo remained silent and simply watched Pete's face as he carried her into the house and up the stairs. His jaw worked with tension and his eyes were shadowed with emotion.

In Jo's estimation, the bull had been a little less angry than Pete.

Chapter 7

"Are you feeling well enough for visitors?" Addie cautiously poked her head around the door frame.

"Of course," Jo shifted in bed, but a sharp pain halted her.

"Please don't try to sit up." Shutting the door behind her, Addie quickly waddled in, stilling Jo's movements with a gentle hand. "The doctor said your ribs are severely bruised, if not cracked. He advised us that you should rest as much as possible."

"I'm so sorry to be such a burden," Jo whispered, reluctantly settling back into the soft bed. Not used to accepting help from others, she was unnerved by all of this attention.

"Nonsense!" Addie exclaimed, fluffing the numerous pillows that surrounded Jo. "You are no trouble at all. I'm just sad that you never told anyone that you were injured from the train accident. We would have called a doctor immediately. I hate to think that you have been in pain for these past few days."

Jo couldn't meet Addie's eyes, and her fingers nervously worried the edge of the patchwork quilt spread over her. Shame and embarrassment competed with the rib pain, making Jo thoroughly miserable. "I thought my ribs would heal on their own," she said quietly. "I don't have money for a doctor, and you and Josh have already done so much for us."

"We are blessed to be able to help you and the other girls. I know you didn't want to be a burden, and I understand. However," Addie cocked a brow. "I'm afraid a certain man is not quite so understanding. He's actually part of the reason I'm here right now instead of letting you sleep. Pete is causing quite a stir downstairs. He's been stomping around, waiting for the doctor to leave so he could come upstairs to see you. I insisted that you needed to rest, but I'm afraid I can't hold him off much longer."

"He probably wants to yell at me some more for being a fool," Jo said dryly. She knew she could probably convince Addie that she didn't feel well enough for a visit from Pete, but she also knew she likely never would feel well enough for a confrontation with that man!

"Is Meg okay?" she asked instead.

"She's fine. She also wants to see you, but I think for the sake of everyone else, Pete should go first."

Addie bit her lip as she poured Jo a glass of water.

Jo could tell that she was wanting to say more, which in spite of everything, piqued Jo's curiosity. Had Pete committed some other atrocity downstairs?

Jo gave her an encouraging smile as she accepted the glass and took a sip, waiting for Addie to continue.

Addie drew a chair close to the bed and sat down.

"He was worried, Jo," Addie said softly. "I've never seen him like that."

Jo's hands trembled. That wasn't exactly the confession Jo expected. She hastily set down the glass on the bedside table, not wanting Addie to see how her words had shaken her.

"I think he was more concerned about his bull," Jo quipped, trying to lighten Addie's somber mood.

"No, Jo." Addie's serious eyes met Jo's. "Pete cares about you."

Jo's breath caught. Addie couldn't be right. Jo obviously infuriated Pete. He teased her unmercifully. He did not like her, and she did not like him. Not one bit.

Well, maybe she liked him a little bit if she was totally honest. And maybe he did care for her some. He *had* risked being gored by a bull to save her, but wouldn't he have done that for anybody?

Jo gulped, feeling tears prick her eyes.

What if Addie was right?

Jo felt her body start to tremble and her breathing became shallow with encroaching panic.

But what if Addie was wrong?

At the thought, the trembling only became worse and a dull ache started in the center of her chest. Somehow, she couldn't find a way to blame it on her injury.

It was all just too much.

"Oh, Jo, I didn't mean to upset you," Addie's brow wrinkled in apology, and she clasped Jo's hand in comfort. "I shouldn't have said anything."

A loud knock at the door prevented Jo from responding.

"Come in," she called, hoping her voice didn't tremble too badly. Somehow she knew that Pete stood on the other side of the door.

She brushed the dampness from her eyes and forced a smile Addie's direction.

Sure enough, the door opened, and Pete's tall form framed the doorway.

Jo's forced smile slipped at the weariness she saw in his eyes. He staggered into the room, his eyes traveling the length of her body before resting on her face.

Addie quickly stood to her feet.

"I will go downstairs and get you some tea. Do you care for chamomile, Jo?"

Addie was out the door before Jo could even respond.

"Are you okay?" Pete asked softly. He stood at the end of the bed, hands jammed into his pockets.

"Yes, I'm fine. Thanks to you." Jo cleared her throat nervously. "I guess this confirms in your mind what you have always thought. Women don't belong on ranches."

Something flashed in Pete's eyes. "I wasn't going to say that, Jo."

"What no Josephine?" Jo quipped.

Pete brushed aside her question. "Meg told me what happened. What you did was very brave; facing a bull with nothing but an umbrella."

"Parasol," Jo corrected, then immediately wanted to bite her tongue. Here Pete was being kind to her, and all she could do was respond with sarcasm. But she couldn't seem to stop herself. She wasn't used to Pete being so serious. It completely threw her off. Jo held her breath, waiting for him to respond.

Pete smirked. "Glad to see you haven't lost your fire."

Air left Jo's lungs in a whoosh. She smiled, relieved the

tension was dissipating.

Pete sat in the chair that Addie recently vacated.

"Your fiancé probably doesn't know it yet, but he is a very lucky man."

Just like that the tension returned, crackling the air.

"Thank you."

Pete leaned forward, close enough that Jo could see flecks of deep sapphire in his icy blue eyes.

He paused, scanning her eyes as if looking for something. His lips parted and words came out in a low, breathless whisper. "He doesn't deserve you."

Jo wet her lips. "You don't even know him," Jo said, her voice equally breathless.

"Don't have to."

"He owns a ranch." Why did she throw that out there? Probably because Pete's nearness was robbing her of the ability to think clearly.

Her somewhat random statement relaxed the tension just a bit, and Pete leaned back, crossing a leg over one knee and remarking casually, "I'm sure he does, if he's from around these parts."

Still feeling nervous and off-kilter, more random words came spewing from Jo's mouth before she could stop them. "He says he has several hundred acres with a thousand head of cattle. And a lovely ranch house."

Pete nodded agreeably, as if these facts were to be expected. "Don't imagine there were a lot of ranches up North. The wife of a Texas rancher might be a hard hat to wear if you've only had frilly, city contraptions on your pretty head before. What did your previous husband do?"

Jo's mind swirled trying to interpret what Pete was saying.

But at that final question, cold trickled down her spine. "Robert Franklin was a banker."

"A wealthy banker?"

"Yes," Jo fidgeted with her fingers, knowing what Pete would ask next. Either he would remark on her lack of qualifications for life on a Texas ranch, or worse, he would commence interrogating.

He did not disappoint.

"Then why are you here?" Pete asked bluntly, scratching his head in confusion. "Shouldn't you still be living the fancy Northern life with your late husband's money?"

Jo winced. Pete had gone the interrogation route. "I was his second wife. His estate went to his sons."

"He left nothing to you?" Pete asked as one eyebrow shot up to his hairline, clearly appalled at the thought.

Jo squirmed, suddenly unable to find a comfortable spot on the bed. She tugged at the quilt, pulling it up toward her chin and covering all but the top of her nightgown. "I'm sure he would have left me a little, if he could have." Jo paused, trying to figure out a way to explain her past. Finally, she just blurted, "Ours wasn't a real marriage."

Then, hearing her own words, she blushed crimson, hurrying to explain. "I was young when we married, and eager to leave my home life. While we didn't have a lot of money growing up, my father worked hard, kept food on the table, and made sure I received a good education. When I was sixteen, he was killed in an accident at the mill where he worked. After that, my mother fell apart, taking up with one man and then another. In order to support us, I was able to procure a job at a bank, where I met Robert Franklin. He was in his sixties and very lonely after his wife had died several years before. When he asked me to be his wife, it was as if someone had thrown me a rope. I could get away from my mother's lifestyle and not be a burden to my older, married siblings. So I agreed."

"And your mother?"

"My husband agreed to grant her a small monthly stipend, but she passed away the month after we married."

Pete frowned. "None of that explains why he didn't leave you any money."

Jo sighed, resigning herself to reporting the entire tale. "Robert had children who were older than I was, and they were unanimously opposed to our marriage. He was just interested in companionship. He wanted someone to talk to, but I think I held a little more appeal because his family objected so vehemently. He married me anyway, but not before they made him legally sign a document stating that I would get none of the family wealth. I think Robert's intention was to make some other investments in my name after our marriage, in order to provide for me. But his health failed shortly after we married. He was no longer able to work as a banker, and everyone thought he would pass away. However, he did not. I took care of him, and though his health improved, it was never fully restored. Thus, when he did pass, everything fell to his children, exactly as stipulated prior to our marriage."

Actual sympathy shone in Pete's eyes. "How long did you care for him before he passed?"

"Twelve years."

"Twelve years!" Pete burst out. "You were married to the man for twelve years and you got nothing? His kids didn't give you even a little?"

Jo shrugged. "They never liked me. They paid for a room for me for a few months until I figured out what I was going to do. That's when I saw the ad for mail order brides. Since I didn't really have any other options, I was matched up with one of the men and agreed to be one of the brides for Perdition." Jo flashed Pete a sad smile. "I did get to keep my clothes."

"You should have just had your own kids," Pete grumbled. "Then they would have to share the money."

As if realizing what he'd just said, Pete's cheeks took on a pink tinge Jo would have found amusing, if her own rosy cheeks didn't happen to match his at the moment.

Jo looked down, studying the various fabrics comprising the quilt instead of risking Pete's gaze. She had come this far in telling him her life story, she might as well admit all the ridiculous details too. "I wasn't exaggerating when I said ours wasn't a real marriage," she said quietly. "There was never an opportunity for children between Robert and me. He was only ever interested in companionship. I think he was forever in love with his dead wife. And I was fine with our relationship at the time. It was a friendship, and I couldn't see him ever as anything other than the fatherly sort."

Pete face was clouded in confusion, and he stumbled, "So you never… I mean, you were married, but you didn't… "

"Tea time!" Addie said brightly, entering the room with a tray of delicate cups, saucers and cookies.

She set the tray on the night stand beside Jo and handed both Pete and Jo one of the rose filigreed cups. "I thought I'd wait until you came back down, Pete," Addie said. "I didn't want to intrude, but it's time for me to start dinner. I thought I'd just sneak in and out." Addie turned to Jo. "Now I don't want you to worry about anything. The girls are going to help make dinner, and then Meg will bring you up a tray. You just rest. That is if Pete will let you have a moment's peace."

With one last warning glare Pete's direction, Addie was

gone.

Pete grabbed a cookie off the plate Addie had left and stuffed it into his mouth.

Jo strongly suspected it was his excuse to not return to their previous topic of conversation. But Jo wasn't going to let him off that easily. If he could interrogate her about her past, then she should be able to interrogate him. Judging by his cantankerous disposition and the shadows in his eyes, Jo was quite certain his would be an interesting story as well.

"Now it's your turn, Pete," Jo said with a mischievous lift of an eyebrow. "I answered your questions; now you answer mine."

Pete looked at her warily, the delicate teacup posed inlarge, work-roughed hand.

With a direct gaze, Jo asked, "Who broke your heart, Peter Harding?"

Though he didn't break eye contact, he brought his teacup up to his lips. As if the movement was unconscious, he opened his mouth and took two big gulps.

Then he gagged.

With the force of his choking, the delicate porcelain teacup flew from his hand and landed right on the top of Jo's nightgown. Jo shrieked as warm tea doused her front and trickled down the inside of her gown.

"Tea!" Pete bellowed. "Addie, where's my coffee? I don't drink this devil brew!"

Jo was sure Pete's tantrum could be heard through the entire house and was likely also providing amusement for the horses down at the barn.

Addie's calm voice soon replied, as if from the bottom of the steps, calling up to the disgruntled man. "Pete Harding, it's called 'Tea Time,' for a reason! If you want 'Coffee time,' you can certainly manage that yourself!"

Grumbling, Pete lumbered to his feet, practically knocking the chair to the floor. "Are you okay?" he asked Jo, almost as an afterthought.

"I'm fine," Jo assured. "I think the tea had been waiting on the counter for a while and wasn't hot. I will need to change though."

"I'll send one of the girls up to help you." His face scrunched up, as if gagging again. "And then I'll find me some coffee to wash that awful tea down!"

His feet heavy, he stomped out of the room without another glance Jo's way.

Obviously, Pete's "Coffee Time" was preferable to answering any of Jo's questions about his mysterious past love. However, Jo was not to be deterred, and before Pete's feet had trounced to the bottom step of the staircase, she was devising plans of how she could procure the information she desired.

Chapter 8

"Addie, please tell me about Pete," Jo requested. If she could have, she would have snatched the words out of the air as soon as they left her lips. She was desperate, but she didn't want Addie to know that!

"Pete doesn't like tea," Addie supplied easily from her seat beside Jo's bed.

Jo smiled, but looked down in embarrassment. "That isn't exactly what I meant," she confessed softly.

Jo felt Addie's eyes on her, examining her closely.

"What about Pete do you want to know?" she asked warily.

Jo bit her bottom lip, trying to think how best to word her request for information she really had no business knowing. Maybe she could have been more patient if it hadn't been days since she had even seen Pete. Addie insisted Jo stay in bed despite her protests, which provided way too much time for her active mind to do nothing but draw endless circles.

She'd had no chance to enact her plans for interrogating Pete, and now she was beyond frustrated. Of course, her potential interrogation might have been the very reason Pete stayed away. Jo didn't want to think of the alternative option that explained his absence—that Addie was wrong: Pete simply didn't care, so he didn't visit. That possibility sucked the air from Jo's lungs and hurt her far worse than her bruised ribs.

Deciding that being blunt was the best course of action, Jo took a deep breath and flung the words out, "Who broke Pete's heart?"

Hearing her own words, Jo flushed in embarrassment and longed to bury her head in the pillows. What was she doing? She had a fiancé! And his name was not Pete Harding! She had no right to feel anything toward a man when her hand was already promised to another.

But she couldn't seem to help herself. He had gotten under her skin. Broken down walls she had erected. He was so unlike Robert. He kept her constantly off-balance. She was normally so controlled. She hadn't lived a privileged childhood, but Robert always remarked that her manners were those of a gently-bred woman. Jo had worked hard to bury her temper, and with such a mild-mannered, older man as a companion, it had been relatively easy to play the part, so much so that she'd almost forgotten who she really was. But Pete had broken down her façade, and yet he seemed to appreciate her fire, as he called it.

Jo sidled a glance Addie's direction. There was no use trying to remedy the situation. By Jo's bold question, Addie would immediately know that Jo had interest and feelings beyond what was appropriate for an engaged woman.

However, instead of rebuke, Jo found only sympathy in Addie's eyes.

"I'm sorry, Jo," Addie said gently. "I'm afraid that isn't a question I can answer. You'll have to ask Pete yourself. It's his story."

Jo nodded in understanding, but she felt the blush to her cheeks intensify, compounded by the corresponding burn of tears behind her eyes. She felt ashamed, embarrassed, and completely lost.

What was she going to do? Jo kept expecting Addie to tell her the tracks had been cleared and her time at the Bar H was over. Jo should want this. Her chance for a husband and a family of her own were within her reach, but she couldn't help but wish that it was Pete who wanted a mail order bride, not Oscar Pruitt.

It's no use wishing on stars that are not even in the sky, Jo thought glumly. Pete didn't want a wife. He made that clear. And now, Jo thought it equally clear that Pete was still in love with whoever it was who broke his heart. Even if Jo could offer an unfettered heart, Pete had no room for her in his.

Addie patted her hand. "Why don't you get some rest?" She wiggled her eyebrows, a hint of orneriness playing about her expression. "It looks like a storm is coming in, so I doubt the men will be busy this evening. I might be able to finagle a way to send Pete up here after dinner. If you're set on interrogating Pete, you'll need all the rest you can get!"

Jo managed a grateful, yet sad, smile. If Pete didn't want to come, none of Addie's "finagling" would do any good.

Addie left and Jo settled back into the pillows. Her eyelids slowly closed as her mind drifted off towards sleep, the image of Pete's dark hair and blue eyes fluttering across her eyelids.

Loud shouts from downstairs violently startled Jo from her

doze. She lurched straight up in the bed with her heart pounding and tender ribs protesting.

Something was terribly wrong.

Jo heard a door slam. Was that Addie crying?

When Pete's name floated to her ears, Jo sprang out of bed. With a hand around her bound ribs for extra support, Jo hurriedly threw a robe over her nightgown before opening her door and rushing to the stairs.

Jo spotted Meg looking out the front window. Pausing at the top of the stairs, she demanded, "Meg, what's happening?"

Meg spun. "Jo! You shouldn't be out of bed!"

"I heard shouting. What's going on?" Jo would not be placated. She wasn't an invalid. If she'd had her way, she would have been out of bed long before now anyway!

Meg glanced out the window one last time before climbing the stairs to meet Jo. "Let me take you back to your room."

"Meg, stop!" Jo batted her hand away. "Tell me."

Meg's shoulders fell in defeat. "There's been an accident. I didn't want you to worry. But Clint went for the doctor."

"Who's hurt?" Jo whispered. Her heart clenched, dreading Meg's answer.

Meg's big doe eyes filled with tears. "Pete."

Jo flew down the stairs, heedless of her attire or Meg's pleas for her to stop. In a few bounds, she was at the front door, wrenching it open and dashing out into the gloomy evening.

Lightning flashed in the distance. Gray storm clouds hovered on the horizon, further darkening turbulent skies. Over the past few days, storms had periodically dumped torrents of rain, making the task of clearing the train tracks even more time-consuming and difficult. Now from the look of the angry clouds, the sky was about to let loose another round.

Jo stood on the porch, trying to ignore the lightning as she frantically glanced to the left and then right, searching for some clue as to where to go.

Storm or not, she had to find Pete.

Voices traveled on the wind, and Jo took off from the porch, her long, unbound hair streaming behind her like a dark cape. Everyone must be behind one of the buildings.

"Addie!" Jo yelled, barreling toward a small group of figures huddled at the end of the barn, not far from a wagon.

"Jo!" Addie exclaimed, catching her friend by the shoulders as Jo slid to a stop in the mud. "What are you doing here? You should be inside."

"Meg said Pete was hurt."

Jo moved past Addie, desperately searching the small group for one tall figure in particular. Pete wasn't there. In fact, there was only one man, the old grizzled ranch hand cook, whose name Jo couldn't remember. The other two people were women, Sadie and Amelia.

The old cook was holding the reins of the horse who was harnessed to the wagon. The horse stamped its hooves and threw its head wildly while the man tried to soothe it.

"Where is he? Where is Pete?" Jo demanded.

Addie obviously didn't want to answer, yet her gaze was nonetheless drawn to the ground beneath the wagon. At the direction of her gaze, Jo's heart plummeted even further.

There was a body under the wagon.

Jo stepped forward. She blinked, hoping to dispel the image.

Addie grabbed for Jo's hand, but Jo shook her off.

"Jo, you must go back to the house," Addie insisted. "You don't even have shoes on."

She didn't have any clothes on either, other than her nightgown and robe, but Jo pressed forward anyway.

As if once again drawn toward Pete by his invisible fishing line, Jo stumbled through the mud, landing on her hands and knees. She crawled the last few feet, oblivious to the rocks and grime that quickly coated her clothing.

Reaching the wagon, she strained her eyes to make out the figure beneath the wooden frame. Pete lay motionless, his face and the rest of his body so splattered with mud that he resembled a mound of dirt more than an actual man. His hat was long gone, and even his dark hair was obscured by layers of dirt that reached to his ears.

"Pete," she called, her voice cracking with emotion. She stretched one trembling hand under the wagon to brush against his arm, fearful that he was already gone from this world.

Pete turned his head, his eyes widening in surprise.

"What in the Sam Hill are you doing out here, Josephine?!"

Jo couldn't stop the smile that broke across her face. "You're not dead."

Pete quirked an eyebrow, his blue eyes twinkling in sharp contrast to the brown of his surroundings. "Disappointed?"

Jo could only shake her head. She was too overcome with relief to form any words.

"Pete, don't move!" Josh's face appeared on the opposite side of Pete. With the wagon blocking him from view, Jo hadn't seen him when stumbling up to the scene.

Josh must have seen Jo startle with instant panic at his words, and he rushed to assure, "He's okay, Jo. Or he will be if he would just stay still." Josh shot Pete pointed look.

"What happened?" Jo asked shakily, not sure if she could trust either man's evaluation of Pete's condition. After all, he was lying motionless under a wagon!

"I was working on fixin' a loose board on the front of the wagon. That fool horse must have seen a bolt of lightning and startled. I was knocked over, and before I could roll out of the way, the wheel was on top of my leg. If Josh hadn't been right there to stop the horse, she would have run me clean over with the wagon!"

"His leg is trapped under one of the front wheels," Josh explained. "If he moves, the metal of the wheel will shred his skin, or break his leg. Right now, his leg is cushioned deep in the mud. We need to lift the wagon off of him, but we don't have enough men to do that. Most of the ranch hands are either helping clear the tracks or out rounding up some of our cattle, too far away to be of any use. I sent a rider for help."

"I'm fine, Josh," Pete grunted. "I can wiggle around and slither out of here myself. We don't need to wait for no one."

"No, Pete," Josh said firmly. "We will wait."

"I don't know 'bout that, Josh," called the old cook. "This here horse is still not takin' no shine to the lightnin'. She's bout ready to bolt."

"Hold him, Hank," Josh ordered. "I will be right there. Pete, don't move."

"Josh, there is a storm comin'. Jezebel is scared of thunder and lightning. She'll bolt at any time," Pete said, moving his arms as if to gain leverage. "I can get out."

"Not without losing your leg. It's not worth the risk."

"Can't you unhitch the horse?" Jo offered, trying to come up with a solution.

"She isn't calm enough for that," Josh explained. "The movements of trying to unhitch a crazed horse could cause the wagon to shift, especially if she tries to take off before she is free. The slightest motion could mean Pete is done for."

Jo gulped, but Pete didn't seem overly bothered. He still continued trying to elbow his way toward the back of the wagon.

A sharp intake of breath had Josh yelling for him to stop.

"Can we dig his leg out?" Jo asked desperately.

Two sets of blue eyes flashed to her.

Josh shook his head. "If his leg sinks deeper in the mud, so will the wagon wheel on top of it. Any hole we dig for his leg, will also include the weight of the wheel following it."

Jo shook her head. Josh wasn't understanding what she was saying. Knowing there was no way to lift the wagon and no way they could wait for help, she tried again. "What if we dug a little ditch right beside the leg and leveraged the weight of the wheel just long enough for him to roll into the empty hole?"

Josh looked thoughtful. "It's a good idea, Jo, but we still have the problem of not having enough men to hold the weight of the wagon while Pete slips out."

"We may not have many men, but you have yourself and at least three able women," Jo said confidently. "It would just take a couple of seconds for him to be free."

Jo looked to her friends. She knew that, with her injuries, there was no way they would let her help, and Addie was out of the question too. But Meg had joined Sadie and Amelia, and all three were watching the scene with frightened eyes.

"Jo's right. We can do it!" Sadie said, stepping forward with a firm set to her chin.

Meg nodded. "We're stronger than we look, and it will just be a few seconds."

Amelia, though silent, stepped forward too, her eyes saying she was also willing.

A streak of white forked to the ground over the pasture, followed quickly by the crash of thunder.

Jezebel snorted and thrashed. The old cook clung to the reins, trying to placate the frightened horse.

"Do it," Pete ordered, slumping back into the mud.

Jo felt a thrill, followed by immediate panic. They were going to use her idea, which meant that whether it worked or not, whatever happened in the next few minutes would be all her fault.

Chapter 9

Josh took charge, immediately grabbing a shovel out of the back of the wagon and issuing orders. "Jo, you keep Pete calm. Don't let him move until I say. Meg and Sadie, you are going to be on this side of the wagon. We'll use this pole to thread through the wheel and brace it. When I give the signal, you're going to hold your end with everything you got. Amelia and I will be on the other end."

After briefing the women, Josh quickly set to work digging while the women took their positions.

Jo turned back to Pete. Sweat beaded his forehead, and she could tell that the stress and confinement were getting to him. She knew he needed some distraction.

Impulsively, she commanded, "Tell me about her."

Pete moaned, closing his eyes. "You sure don't waste no time, do ya? Did you forget Josh told you to keep me calm?

Not sure this is the most *calming* of conversations."

"I'm keeping your mind off of the situation," Jo reasoned, unwilling to give up. "Now who was she?"

"Josh's mother."

Jo's eyes widened in surprise.

But Pete seemed unaffected by his shocking statement. With a quick glance toward Josh and everyone else, as if he was making sure they were all out of earshot, he continued speaking, no emotion registering on his face. "After the war, my brother, Jake, and I were left with no home to return to. Our parents were dead, and the family plantation in Virginia lay in ruins. To make matters worse, we were not welcomed home by our neighbors. We had chosen to serve in the Union army. That made us quite unpopular in a thoroughly Confederate southern community. Thankfully, our father had been smart and split his money between a northern bank and a southern one, so we wouldn't be destitute should the war go either way. We sold what we could, and hightailed it out of Virginia."

Pete paused, seemingly lost in thought, and Jo wondered if he would continue.

After several seconds, the sound of Josh's shovel working so close seemed to rouse him. "Jake and I often played cowboys when we were younger. We promised each other that once the war was over, we would head to Texas and buy a cattle ranch. I was only seventeen, Jake a few years older, when we set off. We bought this land, but quickly realized we had no clue how to ranch. The Bar H would have folded that first year, and we would have lost everything, if Alejandro Morales hadn't shown up when he did. He had owned a ranch closer to the border, but sold it when his health began to fail. For some reason he took pity on two southerners who knew nothin' about cattle. He brought his daughter, Isobel, with him when they moved to the Bar H."

Pete fell silent again, lost in thought.

"Josh's mother?" Jo gently prodded.

"Yes, she was my age, with long black hair and a beautiful smile. Jake and I both fell over ourselves trying to win her attention. I didn't see it at the time, or I just chose to ignore the truth. She loved Jake. But I was young and I loved her, and when I finally pushed her to decide, she chose my brother."

"Did Jake and Isobel want you to leave the ranch?"

"No. I ran away. I was angry. My pride got the better of me, and I left everything that mattered to me: the ranch, my brother. Isobel."

"You were hurt," Jo reasoned.

"I shouldn't have been," Pete's tone was rough, and it was obvious he thought he deserved no sympathy for his actions. "Isobel had only ever had eyes for Jake. I refused to accept that. Even worse, I became bitter and resentful. As the years passed, it became easier to hold a grudge I had no business creating in the first place."

Pete's voice grew softer, and Jo had to strain to hear. "By the time I would listen to reason, it was too late. My brother was dead. Isobel and Jake needed my help, so I came back to the ranch, but even then I wasn't an easy man to live with. When you've been bitter for so long, I guess it seeps into your skin and becomes a part of you, but that's not a good excuse."

"What happened to Isobel?" Jo asked gently. The story was a painful one for Pete, but she had come this far. Now she had to know how it ended.

"Jake passed away when Josh was fifteen." Pete reported. "Isobel did a wonderful job of mothering Josh and managing the ranch. She was always kind to me, even though I wasn't to her. Then she became sick and passed away two years ago. I made my peace with her, but it was still too little, too late."

"She never remarried?"

Pete winced. "I was the only one she would have likely considered marrying, and I was too much of a fool to give up my bitterness and get out of my own way. I had it stuck in my head that I would always be her second choice, and I didn't like that. I finally came to my senses, but by then, she was dying. I wasted all the years we could have had together. I spent them on bitterness that, in the end, earned me nothing but regret."

"And now, as penance for what you did, you're wasting the rest of your years, not in bitterness, but in regret," Jo surmised.

Pete looked at her sharply. "I never said that."

Jo shrugged. "No, you didn't, but it's obvious you feel that way. You're still angry. You dislike women, and won't let anyone get too close."

"Maybe I do feel that way," Pete gritted out. "But I may not be so cantankerous if a certain woman didn't muddle around where she wasn't wanted."

Jo felt the sting, even as Pete cringed at his own words.

With even more regret in his eyes, he tried, "Jo, I didn't—"

"It's starting to rain," Josh announced. "In another three minutes, it's going to be a Texas downpour. If we're going to try this, it has to be now. Already, it took me at least twice as long as it should have to dig this trench. The ground is so saturated that you scoop out the mud, and more mud flows to fill two-thirds of the hole back up. With the rain, it's only going to get worse."

Pete sent one last, long look to Jo, and swallowed. "Ready when you are, Josh."

Josh rushed around the wagon to join Amelia. "Alright,

ladies," he called. "Remember, we don't need to lift the wagon. We just need to support the weight for a couple seconds while Pete slides out."

Jo's heart thumped as she looked from Pete, to Josh and the ladies, and back to Pete. Pete wasn't even looking for her, but was completely focused on waiting for the signal.

She wished she could do something to help!

Lightning flashed again, causing Jezebel to violently swing her neck back and forth. The storm was almost directly overhead, and by the wild look in the horse's eyes, the animal wasn't planning to stick around and watch.

Jo felt large, wet drops nestling in her hair and sliding down her robe. It was as if the storm was right on the edge, holding its breath before letting loose its full fury.

What if this didn't work?

It was Jo's idea. But if the other women couldn't hold the weight, or if the mud gave way beneath Pete, or if he made one wrong move… then the man would never walk again.

Please, God! Jo prayed. *Let it work! Help the women hold the wagon, and keep Pete safe!*

Josh counted. "3… 2…"

"Wait a minute," Sadie interrupted. "Are you going to say '3, 2, 1,' and then go, or are you going to say '3, 2,' and we go on '1'?"

In the space of Josh's silence, Jo could feel the tension radiating off him.

"How about I say, '3, 2, 1, go,' and we go when I say 'go,'" Josh gritted out. "Pete, When I say 'go,' you hightail it out of there."

"Got it," Pete grunted.

Sadie and the other women nodded, but looked nervous.

Poor Amelia looked like she might faint. Once again, Jo hopelessly wished they had more help!

But with the rain quickly increasing, they couldn't wait. It was all up to Josh and the mail order brides.

All Jo could contribute was prayer. She told herself it would be enough. It had to be.

Lost in prayer, Jo missed Josh's countdown, rousing when he yelled, "Go!"

The wagon squeaked.

"Umph!"

"I'm out!"

Two seconds after Josh's initial command, it was over. The wagon creaked backed down in the mud, and Jo rushed around to the side where Pete lay in the muddy ditch alongside the wagon wheel.

She bent to her knees and began wiping off Pete's muddy face with the sleeve of her robe.

Not wasting any time, Hank quickly led the frightened horse to the barn.

"Can you walk, Pete?" Josh asked from behind Jo. "We need to get you inside to make sure your leg isn't injured. I think Addie is already at the house, making coffee."

"Well, I'm pretty sure my leg is still attached, so I think I can make it," Pete said confidently. "And as long as she has coffee and not tea, I suppose I can stop by the house before heading back to the bunkhouse."

Josh helped pull Pete upright, and they all breathed a sigh of relief when, like a brand-new colt, Pete stumbled to his feet.

"If you're real nice to Addie, she might let you borrow her big tub to get cleaned up," Josh said, watching carefully as Pete took his first few steps. "This isn't exactly the weather for a dip in the creek."

After watching Pete gain his footing, Josh rushed on ahead with the other ladies to get things ready for Pete's arrival at the house.

Jo stayed with Pete, keeping pace with his slow gait. Though he didn't seem seriously hurt, he was obviously in pain. Jo hoped the doctor would arrive soon to make sure his leg received the best care.

By now, the rain fell in pelting sheets, though Pete didn't seem at all hurried to get to the house. In fact, he almost seemed to be stalling, as if he was struggling to say something and couldn't quite find the words.

Finally, ten steps from the door, his steps slowed even more and he cleared his throat. "Like I said," he said softly, as if they were picking up right in the middle of a conversation. "When you've made so many mistakes and lived with anger and regret for so long, it becomes a part of who you are."

Jo recognized this as his apology for his earlier harsh words. She also realized it was his crutch, his excuse, for not giving himself permission to live beyond his mistakes.

Thoughtfully, she replied, "My father was a very devout, Christian man, as was Robert. I don't pretend to be a saint; we both know I have too much of a temper for that. But my understanding is that if you ask God for forgiveness, then he is able to pardon you for your mistakes. A life sentence, whether it be in this life or the next, is no longer required for penance."

Pete stared at her, his blue eyes somehow catching the light of the house, even through the pouring rain.

As if in a trance, Jo reached up and gently caressed the mud from his cheek. How could a man be so appealing, even when completely covered in mud?

Pete wasn't going to respond, and maybe that was okay,

for now. Jo had no claim on him, but if she could help him heal by giving him something to think about, then maybe that would be enough.

With a quirk of a smile, Jo deliberately broke the spell and turned to the house. "Come on, I'll pour you a cup of hot tea," she said, leading the way to the door."

"Coffee!" Pete immediately growled.

"Whatever," Jo flung back flippantly. Then, like a proper lady should, she held the door open for the mud monster of a man.

Chapter 10

"You're looking a bit cleaner than when I saw you last," Jo said, walking up to where Pete sat on the riverbank with a fishing pole in hand.

Pete glanced up at her before returning his gaze to the water. He nodded. "I cleaned up best I could last night, and then finished up the job with a dip here in the river this morning before anyone was awake. Unlike some people, I prefer to bathe without an audience."

Jo felt a traitorous blush start at her neck.

Pete sidled a glance up at her again. "I don't suppose you need to use the facilities again? If so, I'd like a little warning so I can make myself scarce. I don't have many more lucky fishing hooks to spare."

Instead of a blush, Jo felt as if a fire raged on her cheeks. "No," she said innocently, as if she had no clue to what he was referring. "I took care of that last night with Addie's tub. I just wanted to see how you are doing. Josh said you were here fishing since the doctor ordered you not to do any work for a few days."

Pete grimaced. "I agreed to one day. That's all."

Jo noticed his leg was at an awkward angle from the rest of his body, as if it was painful and he couldn't find a comfortable position.

"I'm glad it wasn't broken or cut," Jo said, "But you should give it some time for the severe bruising to heal."

"I'm fine. I'll get some fishing done today and get back to work tomorrow."

Jo sat beside him on a patch of soft grass and leaves. Thankfully, Abby had let her borrow a work dress, and it was a relief to be able to sit down without worry of soiling something fancy. She could already tell that she was going to need new clothing when she arrived at her fiancé's ranch. Most of the clothing she had kept from her marriage would not be at all suitable for life on a ranch.

When she arrived at her fiancé's ranch…

Jo smothered a sigh. She should be eagerly waiting for the track to be cleared. She should be excited to start her new life with a husband who wanted her. Instead, she was here. With Pete.

She didn't know what to say, or even what she expected to accomplish by being here, but she wasn't ready to leave. It seemed like something needed to be said, especially after yesterday's events and sharing their pasts with each other. But she didn't know what that was.

And apparently Pete didn't either.

Both sat staring out at the river as the water trickled past and the awkward silence lengthened.

Maybe she should just leave. She didn't have another handy wagon with which to trap the man and force him to talk. If silence was all he was willing to offer, maybe he really didn't care. Maybe there truly was nothing more to be said, and searching for some kind of closure between them was pointless.

"How long does it take to catch a fish?" Jo finally burst, unable to stand the tension a second longer.

"You can't set a watch by it," Pete replied, his tone slightly appalled. "It could happen any time. That's what makes it fun."

More silence.

Fun? This wasn't fun at all. It was *awkward*.

Jo picked up a blade of grass and twirled in between her fingers. It was a beautiful day. The sun shining through the trees was at just the right angle to make everything seem soft, as if the harshness of the outside world could not exist in this one secluded spot. Jo just wished that sense of well-being and peace could penetrate the turmoil she felt inside.

"Are you sure there are fish in there?" she burst out again.

"Yes, I'm sure," Pete grumped, obviously offended by her question.

Jo bit her lip. Then, despite her better judgment, she persisted. "But how do you know?"

And the questions kept coming, with her almost helpless to stop as they spilled forth. "How long do you wait? What if you already had a fish and missed it?"

"Haven't you ever been fishing woman?" Pete gasped, completely exasperated. "If there's a fish on the line, I'll know it."

"Well, I haven't been fishing since I was a child," Jo

admitted. "But isn't it possible to have a fish and let it get away?"

Jo had no idea why she cared. But somehow, the art of fishing, and all its implications, was suddenly of utmost importance to her.

Pete sighed, and with an obvious effort at patience, he answered, "As soon as you feel a tug, you know you have a fish on the line, and you give your pole a good jerk. That sets the hook so the fish is caught. Then, you pull it in."

"What if the tug is light or you miss the pull? Wouldn't the fish get away?" Jo remembered what it felt like when she held Pete's pole the other day. She had definitely felt a jerk then, but was it always that way? And somehow, slapping Pete in the face with the fish didn't quite seem like the proper technique for landing it. It seemed too easy for a fish to escape.

Pete shrugged. "Yes, fish get away sometimes, but there are always more fish."

"But not the same one."

"No, sometimes you miss the best ones."

Jo nodded, though Pete's words bothered her more than they should.

Seeing the troubled look on Jo's face, Pete responded, "Look, Jo, the best way to teach you about fishing is to let you do it yourself."

"Really? You'll teach me?" Jo wasn't excited so much at the idea of learning to fish as she was about the idea that Pete was willing to do something nice and teach her.

"Sure," Pete replied good-naturedly. All trace of his earlier grumpiness was gone as he stood to his feet and offered his spare hand to help Jo up. "I'll teach you proper fishing technique, but since this is the only pole I have on me right now, we'll need to share."

As soon as Jo stood to her feet, Pete handed her the pole. She took it, but held it out from her body at an awkward angle, as if it came with a particularly disgusting odor.

She heard Pete chuckle under his breath. "Jo, you need to hold the pole firmly or a fish the size of a minnow will be able to yank it out of your hands."

Coming behind her, he reached his arms around and grasped her hands in his large, calloused ones, showing her how to wrap her fingers around the pole tightly and hold it close to her body.

Jo felt his solid chest at her back and could hardly breathe, let alone think!

Seeming oblivious to Jo's distress, Pete instructed, "Now, hold the pole still. When you feel a quick yank on the line, give a little jerk of the pole to set the hook. Then use the reel to draw the line in. This is one of the newer, fancy reels. See how smoothly it glides?"

Jo nodded automatically, hoping her mind had recorded enough of the instructions to react properly if a fish actually got on her line. She didn't think she'd be able to consciously make her body do anything, not with Pete so close that his breath whispered in her ear and sent chills down her back!

Pete fell silent, and Jo expected his arms to drop from around her and him to back away. But he didn't. His hands slipped from hers, but perched gently at her waist. Jo felt their warmth seeping through her dress and spreading like a liquid through her entire body.

She kept herself straight as a fence post, but longed to lean into the strength of his torso at her back. The air filled with tension, and Jo felt as if she was being helplessly drawn toward something she couldn't escape, even if she wanted to.

And they waited.

Jo didn't know what they were waiting for, but it seemed even the slightest whisper would ruin everything.

Were they waiting for a fish... or something else?

Then suddenly she realized, none of this was about fishing at all. Her silly questions about fishing, her excessive emotions about whether or not a fish could get away—they were because, deep down, she longed for Pete to catch her!

Pete had once hooked her literally. But if she was his figurative fish, now she was desperately afraid that he would let her get away. After all, he had done so before with Josh's mother. He'd admitted that he'd been too late to seize what they could have had. And despite everything—despite that the man aggravated her to no end, despite that she already had a fiancé—she wanted Pete to pursue her, catch her, and not let her get away.

She knew she'd already put up a fight and wasn't an easy catch, but she wanted him to fight back for all he was worth. She wanted to be wanted, and to be deemed worth the battle of reeling her in.

Was Addie right? Did Pete care for her? Was it enough?

Helplessly, Jo felt her body lean back into him. His warmth and strength seemed to enfold her, making her feel both safe and desired. She felt his breath tickling her neck as he drew her closer. She turned her head to find his face so close to hers. Her eyes traced the strong planes of his face, the rough stubble of a few days break from shaving, his blue eyes, smoldering with an attraction she knew must be reflected in her own.

His lips...

Maybe if their lips touched, maybe then they'd both know.

The pull was too strong. Her eyes slid shut. She felt his

warm breath.

Her lips tingled in anticipation, waiting, longing for the feel of his lips on hers…

The pole, still held securely in her hands, suddenly yanked.

Jo gasped and automatically gave a mighty jerk to the pole, right over her shoulder, just as Pete had instructed.

It was perfect, the end of the long stick landing a direct hit to Pete's head!

Pete yelped, immediately dropping his hold on Jo and cowering from further attack.

"I have one! I have one!" Jo shrieked, frantically reeling the line in. But her efforts were a bit too exuberant. Between the rapid reeling and repeatedly flinging the end of the pole up, the fish didn't stand a chance. Before it could reach the bank in a proper manner, Jo flung the fish up and out of the water, where it conveniently came off the hook and sailed right at Pete's head!

Not to be done in by a fish to the face a second time, Pete ducked. The fish sailed over his head and flopped down in a pile of leaves.

"I got him! I got him!" Jo said, hopping up and down excitedly.

Pete grunted, making repeated swipes at the fish, each time inadvertently knocking it closer to the shore.

"Get him, Pete!" Jo yelped. "Don't let him get away!

Finally, a hobbling Pete triumphantly held the dirt encrusted, flapping fish up with one hand, while his other mopped at the dirt and water still being flung in his face.

Jo rushed forward, clapping her hands with the fishing pole still between them. "I caught a fish! And it's HUGE!"

Pete hurriedly thread a long rope-like twine through the

fish's mouth and grinned in spite of the harrowing drama. "Yes, you did. And it's a nice size. It should fill the length of a pan for dinner tonight. You may have used the most unique technique I've ever seen, but it still counts!"

So maybe it wasn't huge, but Jo was still proud! It wasn't the biggest fish she had ever caught, never mind that it was the only one she had ever caught. Well, technically it was the second, but she didn't really count the other time since she was really only holding Pete's pole. This time, she had been actually "fishing."

Pete reached for the pole that was still waving wildly in Jo's excited hands. "Here, let me take that before you injure someone else. You hold the fish."

"I don't think I…" Jo protested, but Pete shoved the stringer in her hand anyway.

The hand-off seemed to give the fish new energy, and it began vigorously swinging back and forth and flapping wildly. Jo tried to grip the stringer tighter, but it was slick. Before she could get a better hold, the stringer was sliding down, and the fish smacked the front of her dress.

She shrieked, instinctively stepping away from the attack of the wild, slimy creature.

The fish landed on the ground and began flopping its way toward the bank.

"Pete, grab him!" Jo yelped.

Hurriedly setting the pole down, Pete bounded up and swiped at the fish.

Even though it was all tangled up in the stringer, its wild movements kept eluding the grabbing hands of Pete.

Pete scrambled, landing on his knees and yet still crawling, continuing to make wild swipes at the escapee.

With one final plop, the fish landed in the water, taking its stringer and Jo's hopes with it.

Instant tears sprang to Jo's eyes, and she turned on Pete. "You let it get away!"

"I did not!" Pete protested. "You're the one who dropped it! You let it get away."

"Well, excuse me!" Jo fumed, putting her hands on her hips. "I did the hard part of catching the fish. I assumed Pete the great fisherman would have enough skills to pick a fish up off the ground!"

"Now wait here, Josephine—"

"Excuse me," a voice said, hesitantly interrupting.

Both Jo and Pete immediately froze, turning eyes onto Clint, one of the ranch hands at the Bar H.

"Miss Franklin," he said, looking at Jo with his hat in hand. "The boss asked me to come tell you the news. We just got word that the train tracks are clear. You and the other ladies are free to be on your way."

Chapter 11

Jo refused to even glance at Pete as she cleared the table. He hadn't spoken a single word to her since Clint had delivered his message at the river. Now it was hours later, and the mail order brides were scheduled to leave early tomorrow morning. The tracks were clear, and like sand seeping through an hour glass, Jo's time at the Bar H was drifting to a close.

And Pete was going to let her go without a word.

She grabbed a platter with a little too much force, almost knocking it off the table. It probably would have fallen to the floor and shattered had Pete's large hand not clamped over it at the last second. He offered it up to her, and she quickly snatched it without a word of thanks. In fact, she refused to meet his eyes and completely ignored the stream of juice that trickled from the leftover roast onto Pete's lap when she tipped the platter during the exchange.

Tears pricked her eyes as she carried the dishes to the

kitchen, but she refused to allow them to fall. Not here. Not now. Not ever.

She sniffed lightly and raised her chin with determination. If Pete didn't feel the need to talk, to even say goodbye, then she didn't either.

She had no business harboring feelings for Pete anyway. She was engaged to another. She should have known it couldn't end well. If he didn't have a problem with her leaving to marry someone else, then he wasn't worth her tears. At least, that's what she told herself.

After sending Addie off to rest, Jo and her fellow brides took over the kitchen duties for the evening. Meg and Sadie were chatting above the clamor of washing dishes, while Amelia took the job of drying, silent yet nodding and smiling in all the correct places of her friends' ramblings.

Jo placed the platter and other dishes on the table beside the rest of the pile to be washed. She began scraping the leftover food from each of them into a bucket to be fed to the pigs.

Jo jumped at the sound of someone clearing his throat.

She whirled around as the girls' chatter abruptly fell silent.

Pete stood in the doorway to the kitchen with his hat in hand and an unmistakable stain of roast juice streaking down his shirt and pants.

Shifting from one foot to another, he cleared his throat again. "Miss Jo, might I have a word with you on the front porch?"

Wide-eyed, Jo mutely nodded, cleaned her hands on a towel, and moved to follow Pete out, refusing to acknowledge the unabashed looks of delight and curiosity on the faces of the other women.

The screen door on the porch screeched with protest, and

then fell silent with a solid *thunk* behind them. Jo stood beside Pete, looking out at the ranch as if vitally interested in the scene before them. But it was dark, and in reality, Jo could not see past the front steps illuminated by the kerosene lamp in the front window of the house.

The silence was awkward, broken only by the creaking of the porch as Pete nervously shifted his weight back and forth. Though unsure if his movement was from pain or nervousness, Jo got the distinct impression that he was trying to work up the courage to say something.

She felt almost sick with her racing thoughts of what it may, or may not, be.

Just when she feared he would never speak, he rasped, "Jo, there's somethin' I've been meaning to talk to you about."

She waited.

When he still failed to continue, she offered a pointed, "Yes?"

"Well, you know I think that perhaps God might have reason for your train derailin' so close to the Bar H."

"You do?" Jo asked in surprise.

Pete nodded his head, but he still wouldn't look her direction. All his words were spoken to the darkness. "I don't pretend to know all of His ways, but I think that you might be a godsend."

"Really?" Jo asked, her voice practically squeaking. As incredulous as it seemed, she couldn't stop the flare of hope. Did he care for her as she did for him?

"I know we got off to a rough start," he doggedly continued, now warming up to the topic. "But you've proven you are a strong woman, and I think you should stay here at the Bar H."

Finally, he turned to face her, his eyes searching to gauge her reaction.

Jo's heart swelled with the hope that could no longer be snuffed, and she couldn't help the smile that tugged at the corners of her mouth.

"You want me to stay at the ranch?" she asked breathlessly.

Pete nervously rumpled his hat back and forth between his hands. Jo worried that the poor thing would never hold its shape again.

"Well, yes," he said, looking at her in all sincerity. "I guess I do. I think you belong here."

A bright smile lit Jo's face.

Pete returned the smile as he reached out his hand and softly touched the bottom of her chin with his rough thumb. But instead of a caress, he kind of tweaked it, as one would do to an adorable child. "You have quite the temper, Josephine Franklin, but I think you're just ornery enough to make it at the Bar H. The good Lord knows we could use your help."

"We?" Jo's forehead creased in confusion. As Pete's wife, Jo fully intended to help out at the ranch in any way she could, but something about the way Pete said "we" made her wonder exactly what he meant.

"Yes," Pete said, nodding with satisfaction. "I know Josh was lookin' for a woman to come help out at the ranch. I'm sure both he and Addie will be relieved to know they can hire you."

Jo blinked. Did he just say what she thought he'd said?

"You're offering me a job?" she spat out.

"Yep, I sure am," Pete said proudly, not noticing that his words killed both the light in Jo's eyes and the smile on her face. "Addie's gettin' close to delivery, and as you know, there ain't any other women on the ranch. I'm sure she'd appreciate the help and the company."

Help and company for Addie? Was that all she was to him? She wanted to be his wife, not the hired help!

Completely clueless as to Jo's emotions, Pete excitedly continued. "There's plenty of room in the ranch house. You can keep the bedroom you're stayin' in now, and help out with the cookin' and house work. We can talk wages with Josh, but the Bar H pays the best in these parts."

"That's very generous of you," Jo managed, her tone tight with sarcasm as the words barely squeezed around the large lump in her throat.

Her heart was breaking. And it was her own fault. She had been wrong to allow herself to have feelings for a man when she was already promised to another, even if she'd never met her fiancé.

Oh, she had tried not to fall for Pete. He made her angrier than any other person in the world. But he also made her feel—something she hadn't done much of in twelve years. Or her whole life, if she was being honest. Yes, he was cantankerous, but he was also kind, thoughtful, God-fearing, strong, and a hard worker. Pete was every inch a man, and despite her best efforts, Jo had been helpless to prevent the feelings that she had never before experienced.

But apparently her feelings weren't reciprocated.

Jo had spent most of her life being too busy taking care of others for her to live her own life. First her mother, then Robert, and now Pete wanted her to take care of Addie. He wanted her for an employee, not a wife.

And just like that, Jo's ire sparked to life. Piercing Pete with a glare, Jo straightened her spine, stood up straight, and squared her shoulders.

Pete swallowed and shifted a step back, his expression suddenly unsure and confused. He looked at Jo warily, readying for an onslaught that was sure to come.

"And what of my fiancé?" Jo gritted out. "What will I say to him?"

"I'm sure he will understand," Pete's forehead momentarily smoothed, as if relieved that Jo's objection was just a minor detail. "Josh and I will reimburse him for any money he spent on your travel. I can send him a wire when I take the other ladies to the train. What was his name again?"

"That won't be necessary," Jo replied brusquely. "I don't think money will suffice, in this case. Oscar Pruitt wants me for his wife. Not an employee."

Pete's head snapped back as if he had been slapped.

Jo met Pete's shadowed gaze, and with a firm voice, she spoke in no uncertain terms. "I will not be a hired hand, Peter. I've lived that life before. I won't do it again."

Pete stepped closer, his eyes flashing. "And you would prefer Oscar Pruitt's company to… the Bar H? You don't even know this man, Josephine."

"Apparently I don't know you either," Jo snapped. "I thought you were more intelligent than to think a woman would want to spend her life as your employee. I thought you might be able to move on. But I guess I was wrong."

"Be reasonable, Josephine." Pete tossed his hat on the porch railing and set his hands on his hips. "This man could be dangerous."

"And you are not?" Jo matched his pose, placing her hands on her hips and fixing him with a glare that could make a preacher cower. "I think you are far more dangerous than he is. You are promising me nothing. Hard labor on a ranch and decent pay? What kind of life is that? He has promised me a home, Pete."

"You can have a home here," Pete said.

"I am not young, Pete. I want a family before it's too late."

"Josh and Addie will be your family."

"What about you, Pete?" Jo prodded. "Will you be my family as well?"

Pete was silent, his jaw working as he ground his teeth.

"You see, Pete. Oscar Pruitt has promised me himself. Something you will never do."

"Jo—"

"Don't Jo me!"

"Confound it, woman! Give me time! I barely know you! We've only known each other for a few days. Maybe in time we could be more."

"How long do you need, Pete? A month? A year? Maybe two?"

"I don't know," His fingers wore the familiar path through his hair.

"How about 13 years?" Jo whispered. "Isn't that about how long you waited to come back to the Bar H the last time?"

"That's hitting below the belt, Jo."

Jo's anger deflated, and her shoulders sagged. "I know, and I'm sorry. But Pete, please be honest. You aren't ready for anything more than an employee, and you may not ever be."

"Jo, I don't know. I can't make you any promises. Not with my past. You know that."

"Then I'm sorry, Pete. But If you can't make a promise, then I most certainly can't break mine. I'm going to Perdition."

And with that, Jo turned from him to go inside.

"Jo," he called, stopping her.

Jo paused, but didn't turn back around.

"I don't want to regret you," he said, his voice strangled with emotion.

"Unfortunately, regret is not enough," Jo replied sadly.

"Then what is it you want from me, woman?" Pete burst out.

Jo closed her eyes in pain, still refusing to face him. "Apparently I want something you cannot give," she said softly.

Without another word, Jo entered the house, letting the screen door fall shut on the man she loved, and his regret.

Chapter 12

Perdition, Texas

"Well, ladies," Sadie said. "We finally made it."

Jo stepped down from the train, the last to disembark behind the other three women. Somehow she had wanted to delay the inevitable, to pretend that she hadn't left the Bar H—and Pete. That they hadn't taken the train to Perdition. That her fiancé wasn't waiting for her.

She turned and looked longingly back up the steps as if she could see through the route they'd just traveled, back to the ranch.

But it was useless. Pete didn't want her anyway. She hadn't seen him since their argument last night on the porch. Josh had been the one to wake up early and drive the brides to the station to collect their luggage before boarding the train for Perdition.

Jo raised her chin with resolve. She had no choice but to make the best of things. Her future was not back at the Bar H. It was here. And the sooner she accepted that, the sooner the pain in her heart would go away, at least that is what she told herself.

Sadie spun in a slow circle. "So this is Perdition, Texas. I'm not going to lie, the name kinda fits. It sure is not too much to look at, is it?"

Meg and Amelia murmured their agreement, while Jo adjusted and readjusted her gloves, trying to pay no heed to her surroundings. But it was more than a little hard to ignore.

Whereas Last Chance hadn't been the most picturesque, there were still trees and the buildings were arranged in a semblance of order. The Bar H had actually been pretty with its acres of rangeland and the small river running through the center. But Perdition wasn't pretty or picturesque. It was desolate.

Dust blew down what Jo assumed was a street, but since the rough-hewn buildings looked like pieces of trash thrown across the flat dirt in a haphazard manner, she couldn't be sure. This wasn't exactly some place she'd ever envisioned calling *home*.

Jo swallowed and struggled to keep the burning behind her eyes from spilling over in tears. She had to get her emotions under control. She was going to meet her fiancé today. She had to forget Pete Harding and what might have been. That's all there was to it. This was reality. She had a hard time imagining she could ever be happy in a place like this, but she could learn to accept it.

"Well, let's see if we can find our grooms, shall we?" Sadie led the way with Meg toward the small building that resembled more of a shack than a train depot. Amelia slowed so that her gait matched Jo's.

"Are you okay, Jo?" she whispered. "You haven't been quite yourself since... well, last night."

"I'm fine."

"Are you sure?" Amelia asked, peering at her far too intensely. "From the beginning of our journey, you have been our unofficial leader. Now Sadie is the one charging ahead."

"I think Sadie is excited to finally arrive here," Jo replied, trying to casually move the topic off of herself.

"And you aren't?" Amelia probed quietly.

Jo managed a half-hearted attempt at a smile and shrugged her shoulders, not wanting to fully voice the emotions she was feeling.

With a gentle hand on her forearm, Amelia stopped Jo from reaching for the depot door. "If I can do anything for you, or if you want to talk, I am here for you, Jo. I am a good listener."

"I know you are, Amelia. Thank you, but I am fine." Jo spoke sincerely, but couldn't actually meet the compassion in her friend's gaze. Now if her own words about being fine could just convince her heart.

Unfortunately, Amelia didn't look any more convinced than Jo's heart was.

Though hesitant, Amelia's quiet voice persisted. "Jo, if you change your mind, and decide you don't want to marry your groom, please don't."

At her pause, Jo finally looked up, curious at her friend's tone. Jo's gaze met Amelia's sad, honey-brown eyes.

Her voice a pain-laced whisper, Amelia continued. "There are few worse things in life than an unhappy marriage.

Especially if you love another."

Jo's eyebrows shot up in surprise.

With a gentle squeeze of her hand, Amelia released Jo and entered the depot, leaving Jo to wonder what experience had led Amelia to that conclusion.

Thoughtfully, she followed Amelia into the depot.

"Jo, hurry on over here," Meg called, motioning Jo over to the counter. "The station master is helping us locate the men. What was your groom's name?"

"Oscar Pruitt," Jo replied, joining the other women. An older man stood behind the counter. His black trousers and matching vest over a white shirt identified him as the station master, even if Meg hadn't mentioned anything.

"Oscar Pruitt!" He exclaimed, his bushy white brows chasing his receding hairline. "Are you sure?"

"Yes, I am quite certain," Jo said, suddenly uneasy. She reached into her handbag. "I have a letter right here."

The station master took the paper Jo offered, his eyebrows raising an impossible inch more.

What was going on? Jo glanced at the other brides to see if they were as disturbed as she was about the station master's reaction to her fiancé name.

All three wore anxious expressions. Meg stepped closer, placing a comforting hand in hers.

"It does appear to be Oscar Pruitt," the station master admitted reluctantly.

"Do you know where I can find him?" Jo asked boldly, refusing to back down.

"Well, I bet I can guess, but I'm not—"

"Ye lookin' for Oscar?" a voice called from behind them. Jo turned to see a weathered man spit an impressive stream of tobacco juice onto the station floor. "I know where he be. I ken take you on over myself."

"Now, George, you wait," the station master interjected.

"I'm just offerin' to take the lady to Oscar," George said, holding up his hands and stepping away from the corner where he'd been leaning. "Nothin' more."

"You know where he is?" Jo said apprehensively.

"Yep. He's not fer at all. Just around the corner."

"Jo, don't," Meg tightened her hold as Jo moved to follow George. "Something doesn't feel right."

"It's okay, Meg," Jo said quietly but firmly No matter what the circumstances, I need to speak with Mr. Pruitt. I will be right back to get my things."

"Miss—" the station master called.

"Don't worry, Martin. I'll make sure she gets to Oscar," George smiled, fully displaying an unusually fine set of white teeth that looked quite misplaced on a face matted with grime and overgrown whiskers. "This ought to be a good show."

Jo gulped and followed the man from the depot, not daring to look at the other women for fear she would lose her courage. She knew that something wasn't right, but she also knew she needed to see what it was and talk to Oscar Pruitt herself.

Jo followed the man named George away from the train tracks toward the other clustered buildings that made up the town. There wasn't a boardwalk, just dirt that was a slightly lighter shade than the buildings themselves. There were a few other people on the "street," and they all seemed to give Jo strange looks. Self-conscious, Jo tried to keep her eyes downcast, watching the dust layer her traveling suit and once-clean boots.

Jo tried to be thankful. Dust was better than some things, like manure. And so far she had managed to avoid the periodic shots of tobacco juice flung every which way by her helpful guide.

"What did you say yer name was?" George flung over his shoulder as they neared one of the buildings.

"Jo Franklin," she answered calmly. "Mr. Pruitt should be expecting me. I'm late actually. The train derailment outside of Last Chance delayed all of us mail order brides."

"Mail order bride, eh?" George sneered, stopping at the door to a ramshackle building that boasted no paint, no windows, and no sign out front. "I thought that's what the other women said. Oscar done got himself a bride! Wonder how he done did that!"

"We were matched by an agency," Jo hurried to explain, eager to show that theirs was a legitimate and proper arrangement. Jo reached back into her satchel and pulled out Oscar's letter. "We corresponded and the letter he sent requested I come and included the train tickets."

George tipped his head back and laughed. Then he began coughing and choking on his own tobacco juice.

In between bursts of laughter, he finally managed to open the door to the building and motioned Jo to enter.

Jo, bewildered by his reaction, automatically stepped inside.

"That's a good one!" George coughed, still trying to clear his throat. "Miss Mail-Order-Bride, I don't know who wrote that letter, but it ain't Oscar! Oscar can't even read his own name!"

The instant Jo stepped through the door, she knew she'd made a mistake. Rough hewn tables and chairs littered a large, dark room, and along one side ran a long counter. Both the tables and counter were inhabited by men—only men. And they all seemed to be holding glasses filled with varying shades of amber. At her entrance, all conversation halted, the tinkling sound of glassware was met with silence, and playing cards dropped to the floor. More than a dozen pair of eyes turned her direction.

Jo had just stepped into a saloon.

She froze. "There must be some mistake," she said to George. "I didn't see a sign. I should... um... I'll wait outside."

Jo backed up and whirled to leave, but George was in her way.

He pointedly stood between her and the door, chuckling. "Why would anyone waste good money on a sign when everyone already knows this be the saloon!"

Jo's thoughts whirled with panic. She had no idea what was going on, but all of her instincts were urging her to flee. She tried to wrench her arm away and retreat, but George held her tightly.

"Oscar Pruitt, I got somethin' here that belongs to you!" George called out loudly.

A grizzled man stood from one of the tables.

Jo couldn't breathe. This couldn't be her intended! There must be another Oscar Pruitt! But her frantic eyes didn't find another volunteer standing to his feet.

George grinned and nodded at the heavily-bearded man. "She says her name is Jo Franklin and that she's here to marry your lonesome hide. She got a fancy letter and everything. I guess she be your mail order bride!"

"Well, I'll be." The gruff voice that emitted from the beard was immediately followed by a sneer that sent chills of terror down Jo's spine. His tobacco stained, matted whiskers parted to reveal brown teeth. His beard itself was a mixture of brown and gray, with the gray matching the color of his long, scraggly hair.

Jo shook her head, denying the image that her eyes saw before her.

"Well, boys, what did I tell you! That silver-tongued peddler was true to his word! I be gettin' married!"

Two younger men jumped up and began thumping the older one on the back. "Pa, your fool idea done worked! We thought you crazy for spending' our hard-earned gamblin' money on a mail-order woman. But here she is! And ain't she proper lookin'!"

Oscar Pruitt had children! Well, they couldn't really be labeled children when they were both adults, just as filthy and unkempt as their father!

They came forward, circling around Jo as they would a piece of livestock, inspecting every inch of her. Jo alternately wished she could just melt into the floor and pretend none of this was happening!

One of them dared to reach out and run one dirt-encrusted finger down Jo's cheek. "Ain't she a purty one?"

Jo reached out and slapped his hand away, furiously staring him down. How dare he touch her!

"And feisty too," the other son guffawed.

"Hands off, boys!" Oscar said, casually moving to join his sons clustered around Jo. "That be my woman, bought and paid for, and soon to be your new ma."

"Come on, Pa! There's nothin' wrong with sharin'," the one who had touched Jo protested. "Remember some of that money you stole from us."

"I stole nothin' you hadn't already stolen from me! You

and Clyde could have ordered yer own woman. But you wouldn't believe him when he said his company would take care of all the letters and tickets and such. But I was a believer. I told you he was a proper business man. Sure enough, he was true to his word and sent me a woman, just like he said!"

The one called Clyde laughed. "Pa, you would have never given him the money if you hadn't been fallin' down drunk!"

"Even drunk, I'm smarter than you boys! I'm the one who got me a woman to warm my bed!"

Jo looked around the room, desperately wishing she was anywhere but here. Every man in the saloon was watching the scene with a horrid leer fixed like a mask on his face. They were the show, and with Jo being the main attraction, she knew she would receive no empathy or help from her drunken audience.

It was all up to her.

"I think there's been a mistake," Jo said firmly, finally able to be heard above the men. "I was matched up with a groom by the Western Matrimonial Company. I was told his name was Oscar Pruitt, but since you weren't the man who corresponded and obviously weren't expecting me, I'm afraid there's been a misunderstanding. If you will excuse me, I will send a telegram to Western Matrimonial and notify them of the mix-up."

Jo turned, waiting expectantly for George to move and let her past. When he didn't budge, she began pushing her way. She needed to get out of here.

"Now wait a minute," Oscar said. Suddenly, his two sons were flanking George, and she had no choice but to turn back around from the exit. "I never said I wasn't expecting you, missy. I got me a proper contract from that western bride company about a month after I paid them for you. 'Course, I can't read it, but a friend read it for me and said you were comin'. When you didn't show, I thought I'd been duped for sure by that Baxter and his bride store. Now I know that you were just late and he done did right by me!"

Jo felt her frustration turn to temper. She would have preferred to have this conversation without curious eyes, but she certainly was not going to go anywhere with him! So if he wished to have the discussion here, she wouldn't disappoint!

Eyes flashing, voice barely containing her anger, Jo spoke, "Sir, if what you say is true, if he did 'do right by you, then Western Matrimonial certainly did *not* do right by me! I am the one who has been duped and sent correspondence from a man who didn't write it. I was lied to and manipulated. You are not the Oscar Pruitt I agreed to marry. And I certainly have no intention of marrying *you* as a replacement."

Something changed in Oscar's face. His delighted sneer became fixed and his eyes grew hard. "No matter what fancy words you use or angry fits you throw, it doesn't change that I have your signed name on my contract, Josephine Franklin. I paid for you, and soon as the preacher is free of his duties, you will be my bride, no doubt about that."

"I will not!" Jo hissed back. "The man I am to marry is in his thirties, with no children, owns a ranch outside of Perdition, and is a God-fearing Christian man. That is obviously not you!"

Oscar shrugged. "I can't help what words good ole Baxter put with my name. You agreed to marry Oscar Pruitt, and marry him you shall. Besides, though I haven't seen my thirties in a while or the inside of a church, I do own a ranch."

The entire saloon erupted into laughter.

"Oscar, you own a ranch like I own a castle," George said, shaking his head with a grin. "Your shack and few acres of weeds don't count any more as a ranch than your dogs count as cattle!"

"I don't know, boys. If my bride be wantin' a rancher, we should probably take her out and show her the place. We'll keep her nice and cozy until the wedding this evenin'."

"I will not go with you!" Jo said, adamantly stomping her foot. "Let me go right now or I'll start screaming for the sheriff!"

"Clyde, Elmer, go fetch the wagon."

His sons hurried out the door to obey. Wasting no time, Oscar stepped up to Jo and hoisted her over his shoulder.

Though it was impressive that the older man was able to do so easily, it was more impressive, and entertaining to his audience, when Jo started kicking!

"Let me go!" she screamed, pounding him on the back.

"Yell all you want, Josephine Franklin. There ain't a sheriff or a man in Perdition who would lift a finger against a man taking what is rightfully his!"

"Now wait a minute," George protested, looking unsettled. "If the lady don't want to go, I'm thinkin' the show's over."

Oscar sneered, "What are you gonna do about it, George? Go right ahead and talk to the sheriff. I'm sure he'd like to see you again."

"All ready, Pa," Elmer announced, returning with Clyde in his wake.

George's jaw flexed beneath his overgrown whiskers. "I may not be a popular fella right now in either Last Chance or Perdition. But I can't stand by and let you—"

As if it had been rehearsed, Clyde and Elmer each landed a fist—one to the gut, one to the jaw.

George plopped to the floor.

The saloon erupted in cheers and hoots.

Oscar shook his head. "That George be havin' a bad string of luck. Should have minded his own business."

Without another glance, Oscar and his sons paraded from the saloon with Jo carried around like a sack of flour.

Jo screamed, pounded her hands on his back, and kicked with every bit of strength she had in her. But to the men in the saloon, it was all a hilarious show.

Seconds later, Jo was carried out of the building and to the waiting buckboard wagon. Frantically, she twisted her body, not caring if she fell flat on the dirt as long as she was out of Oscar Pruitt's grasp. But his arms holding her firmly to his shoulders felt like tight ropes.

"Help me!" she screamed, hoping that someone on the street would hear and intervene.

She lifted her head up, trying to find someone who could help her. As she was thrown into the back of the wagon and literally tied down with ropes, her eyes collided with the shocked gaze of Amelia. But her friend was too far away to stop Jo from being kidnapped, even if she could.

With a heart sick with fear, Jo realized that if her groom was not what he'd appeared to be, if Western Matrimonial had deceived her, chances were good that her friends were facing similar difficulties.

A rag was stuffed in her mouth and tied securely so she could only gag instead of yell. The men jumped up on the wagon and slapped the horses into a run. Jo was thrown around the back of the buckboard, quickly losing sight of Amelia and the buildings of Perdition.

She was a prisoner with no one to come to her rescue.

God help us! Jo prayed desperately, knowing that He was the only one who could.

The brides of Perdition were in trouble.

Chapter 13

The rough gag was still in place when the wagon finally rolled to a stop. Though her feet were still tied, Jo scrambled to a sitting position, ready to strike at anyone who came close. She might be bound and gagged, but she was not completely helpless.

"Where we goin' to put her, Pa? She's fighting somethin' fierce back here."

"Throw her in the shed, Clyde. I need a bit of shut eye before I show my new wife around." Oscar winked suggestively at Jo before jumping from the wagon.

Jo fought the nausea that welled in the back of her throat.

"Why me?" Clyde moaned. "I done rode in the back with her all the way from town. She kept kicking me worse than a mule. It's Elmer's turn to deal with her."

"Fine. Elmer, you take her," Oscar waved his hand dismissively as he headed toward what Jo assumed was the house. Although the pile of rough-hewn mismatched boards stacked together with a lopsided door hanging at a precarious angle hardly constituted more than a shack, let alone a house.

"But, Pa," Elmer whined. "My stomach is hurtin' something fierce. I think Old Man Sal's batch of moonshine was bad."

"I told ye not to drink the whole bottle! You deserve whatever befalls you!"

"But, Pa!"

Clyde snickered.

"You hush up here, Brother," Elmer sneered. "I'll pack her out back, but you gotta take care of the horse."

"No way, Elmer, it's your turn!"

"Stop your bickerin', you good for nothin' boys! I been up all night at the tables. A man deserves to have some peace and quiet after workin' a hard day."

"You mean night," Clyde corrected.

Oscar turned, his eyes flashing. "I outta box yer ears, boy."

Clyde visibly gulped.

"Ye both take care of the chores. And be quiet about it, ye hear?"

"Yes, Pa," the boys echoed.

Oscar half-swaggered, half-stumbled to the door of the "house." Swinging it open with a screech of rusty hinges, he then turned back with a grin.

Jo shuddered. Whatever teeth the man had left were thoroughly blackened. The smile was not one of happiness or joy, but seemed to boast an evil anticipation that sent shivers down her spine.

"Preacher should be done with that other weddin' and festivities soon." Oscar nodded to the sun's position, pointing out the time of day. "After I get some shut-eye, we'll head back to town and make things official. A man should be well-rested for his weddin' night. Be ready to leave at supper time, boys! We'll be celebrating your new ma tonight!"

Punctuated by an ominous shriek, the door swung shut behind Jo's fiancé.

Clyde reached out to untie the ropes binding Jo's feet, but it wasn't an easy job. Even as he worked to free her, Jo kicked, twisted, and fought, trying to get away, though if she couldn't escape, she would have settled on just seriously injuring one of her kidnappers.

With a growl, Clyde finally pushed her back down in the wagon, turned her over, and put his knee in the middle of her back, holding her firmly so she couldn't move.

Jo had seen a similar move when one of the ranch hands wrestled a calf down and tied it up for branding. With that knee digging into her back, Jo instantly felt a miserable empathy with the poor animals.

She couldn't breathe. The pressure on her ribs was so painful, she feared she might pass out. She wanted to scream in pain, but couldn't even gather enough air in her lungs to blow away the gathering darkness in her vision.

Every little sensation was intensified. She smelled the hay in the wagon beside her and felt splinters from the rough wood below her bite into her flesh through her dress. A wave of nausea crept up around her, and she was suddenly horribly warm.

She felt a strange disconnect with her body, and seconds seemed to divide themselves into slowly meandering parcels of time. Almost as if she was outside of her body observing, the scratchy ropes left her feet, and she heard them thud back into the wagon.

Then, without any warning, Clyde's knee let up from Jo's back, and she was hauled backward out of the wagon and slung over a dirty shoulder. She sucked in great gulps of air, even as she weakly raised her now-freed feet, ready to use any remnant of strength to pommel the brute who was carrying her.

But Elmer's growl in her ear stopped her.

"I'm warning ye now, Miss, I'm not nearly as nice as Clyde. Ye kick me, I'll hit ye back. Harder."

Jo stilled at the threat, remaining limp as she was hauled over Elmer's shoulder. Up until this point, Jo's anger had drowned out all other emotion. But now, for the first time since being kidnapped, Jo felt a shiver of fear roll down her spine, and on the heels of that fear was outright panic.

She knew she had to get away from these men as soon as possible. She didn't have time to wait for help, assuming someone would come searching for her. Amelia had seen Jo thrown into the back of the wagon, but Jo couldn't count on help arriving. She was on her own.

Jo landed with a painful thump onto hard-packed dirt. Unable to catch herself with her hands still tied, her still-healing ribs took the brunt of the fall.

"If you promise to keep quiet, I'll take the gag out," Elmer offered, though there was no compassion in his tone.

Jo nodded, anxious to get the foul-smelling rag from her mouth. The tight fabric had bruised from her lips to her neck. If she could have any relief from the pain and smell, she would take it.

"How long am I expected to wait here?" Jo bit out, her hoarse voice scratching past her dry throat.

"Pa will most likely sleep the day away. But rest assured, as soon as he wakes up, he will come and get ya." Elmer leered.

Jo tried to keep her expression neutral. She didn't want to give away her determination to escape. *I will be gone long before Oscar Pruitt darkens this doorway,* she promised herself.

But Elmer must have seen something in her face.

"Don't get any ideas of escape. The door is locked. I'm gonna bind some rope around the door to make sure it stays that way. I'm leavin' your hands tied, and if you make too much ruckus, I'll come and tie yer feet up again too, but it will be real tight this time."

With that, Elmer grunted what Jo assumed was goodbye as he slammed the door shut on his way out.

Jo waited for the sounds of Elmer making good on his promise. Sure enough, the sliding sound of rope against wood along with a few strong pulls of the door convinced Jo that one route of escape was not going to be an option.

But Jo refused to let panic take hold. One step at a time. She would get out of this mess. Taking a deep breath, she focused on the rope binding her wrists. Elmer and Clyde had done a fair job of securing them, but Jo's wrists were slim. Slowly, she turned her hands side to side. The rope moved ever so slightly. With determination, Jo continued with back and forth movements of her wrists, refusing to dwell on the burn of the rope as it stripped her tender flesh.

With one last flick of her wrist, the rope slid from her fingers. She had done it! Her hands were free. Jo stifled her whoop of joy, and settled for a quiet smile of satisfaction.

Now all she had to do was find a way out of this shed. Jo took a slow turn around the room. There were no windows, and the only opening was the securely locked door. The small room would have been pitch black except for the dim light filtering in through the cracks in the makeshift roof.

From where she stood, it certainly seemed there was no

escape.

Jo fought the despair that threatened to overwhelm her.

God, help me! she prayed. *You rescued the Apostle Peter from prison, you can surely get me out of Oscar Pruitt's shed!"*

Jo's eyes were drawn up toward the slivers of light in the roof. The entire shed seemed to be built very haphazard. Could it really be that difficult to escape?

Suddenly, she had an idea.

Her gaze flittered around the earthen floor, searching for the equipment she needed for her plan. Unfortunately, there wasn't a lot to work with. Crates filled with empty gin bottles and rotting fruit lined the walls. Broken farm equipment littered the floor.

The shed, as well as the shack the Pruitt's called home, had definitely seen better days, or maybe they'd been built so clumsily that they'd never had better days. She could probably take the rusty saw to the drooping boards and cut herself a new door. But the sound would most likely wake her kidnappers.

Her new plan was better, provided she didn't seriously injure herself.

Ignoring the pain in her ribs, Jo dragged the crates over to the wall. One by one she upended the contents to the floor and stacked them until a rickety ladder formed.

Once the last wooden cases were in place, Jo took a rusty rake and carefully hung it in place against the top crate. Then she gently tested the bottom to see if it held her weight. A slight wobble, but it would hold. She hoped.

No, she shouldn't just hope. Closing her eyes, Jo lifted her chin to heaven and prayed again.

Lord, I need you. Please help me to get out of here and to not get hurt in the process. I don't know that I need an angel to escort me out of prison like Peter, but I do need a way to get permanently away from that evil man and his sons! I don't want to be around him, let alone be his wife!

The more Jo thought about her situation, the more she feared getting out of the shed wouldn't be enough to keep her out of Oscar Pruitt's grasp. *Maybe I do need some extra miraculous help, even if I get out of here. So, if you send me an angel, Lord, I won't turn him away!*

Escaping the shed wouldn't solve all of her problems, but it would at least take care of the immediate one. One deep breath and Jo began her climb. The crates shifted unsteadily beneath her feet. Jo scurried faster. Four bins up, Jo reached out and retrieved the rake from where she had positioned it.

She looked up. She had built her crate tower directly beneath the largest hole in the roof. Now she extended the rake above her head, hoping her plan would work. The roof looked as if it had been assembled with wood scraps and sticks, some of which looked to be in such bad shape they were surely rotten.

Balancing carefully, Jo thrust the handle of the rake up sharply. With a crack, the flimsy wood immediately gave way. More light filled the shed as the hole suddenly got bigger.

Excited, Jo hit the roof repeatedly, making the hole wider with each splinter of wood.

Then she heard the unmistakable sound of someone coming. She froze. Had her work made too much noise? Was Elmer coming to tie her up again?

She held her breath, listening to the sound of footsteps and the odd grunting movements coming closer. A door screeched.

Panicked, Jo's eyes automatically flew to the door below her, but it remained closed.

With another screech, then a thud, whatever door that was opened slammed shut.

All of the air expelled from Jo's lungs in a rush. But the sudden relief of tension startled her precarious balance. The crates below her shifted.

Jo fought to keep them steady, but it was no use. Her arms flailed, trying to find a position that wouldn't topple the tower, but she quickly realized that the only way to keep the crates from crashing was to abandon ship.

Without fully thinking it through, she stepped up to the top crate, put her arms through the hole, and pulled herself through. Jo waited, wincing in anticipation of the deafening crash of crates. But it didn't come. Without her weight, the tower thankfully settled back into its precarious, yet upright, position.

However, after averting one disaster, Jo realized she had only exchanged it for another predicament. What had she been thinking? If the roof was flimsy enough for her to poke through with the handle of a rake, what made her think that it could hold her weight when she climbed out?

Jo's head now stuck out of the hole in the roof, but with each slight movement, she heard the creak and crack of splintering wood. She frantically looked around. How could she get down?

Her eyes landed on the building next to the shed. She was sure this was the one she'd heard someone enter just a moment ago. If she concentrated and listened past her own pounding heartbeats, she could hear the movements of someone inside the tiny building.

It didn't take much imagination for Jo to figure out exactly what kind of building it was. After all, those things were pretty standard. It was slightly shorter than the shed and shaped in a small square. Jo knew that if she actually had a view of that squeaky door, she would likely see a cutout of a half moon positioned toward the top.

It was an outhouse.

Jo wished she could wait until whoever was in the outhouse came out. She would take her chances that they wouldn't notice half her body sticking out of the roof of the neighboring shack.

But that didn't seem to be an option. By the sound of the creaking wood, Jo knew the roof wouldn't hold her for long. She was close to the side of the shed. If she could just make it to where the roof met the wall, then the wood may be better supported and just might hold her weight while she figured out how to get down.

Trying to keep her weight equally divided between her arms, she slowly lifted herself out of the hole. Her torso came out, and she laid flat while trying to pull the rest of herself out. But somehow the steady, gentle pulling wasn't extracting the other half of her body out of the hole.

She tugged harder. And harder. But she wasn't making any progress.

Jo closed her eyes, reluctantly facing the truth. Two sides of the hole firmly gripped her hips.

She was stuck.

She wiggled, gently maneuvering her hips side-to-side.

Nothing.

She wiggled more, kicking her legs as if she could give added momentum.

Still nothing.

She tugged, pulling herself as hard as she could and feeling the wood prick her hips like hundreds of Pete's fishing hooks. She was going to have massive splinters all over after this! That is, if she ever made it out!

Jo bit her lip, feeling tears burn her eyes. Increasingly frustrated, she performed every gymnastic move she could think of, yet she could not get even another inch of her lower body through the opening.

I did not come this far to be stuck in a hole!

And with one last angry burst of desperation, she abandoned all caution and raised her knee up hard, directly into the roof.

The wood gave way, making the opening bigger and allowing her to quickly scramble out.

But the splintering wood didn't stop with the part that Jo knocked with her knee. Crawling across the roof, she felt it giving way beneath her. Each move she made collapsed another piece, her path tumbling below in her wake.

She reached the edge of the building. But she found no safety. The entire roof was collapsing, and it looked as if some of the walls would soon follow. Her eyes darted around, seeking any way down from the roof.

But she was out of time.

Seeing only one option, she gathered her feet under her and made a mighty leap. She felt the wall of the shed give way under her shoes, and she was in the air.

But Jo didn't fall. Instead, her desperate leap landed her safely... on the roof of the outhouse.

Chapter 14

Though Jo's leap landed her on target, she hadn't counted on needing to stay on the roof. Her momentum was too much for the little building, and the force of its new occupant sent it reeling to the ground.

Feeling the outhouse tip, Jo rode it like a bucking bronco, staying in her crouched position and instinctively leaping again right before it hit the ground.

The landing may have been too much for her poor ribs if not for the cushioning of a large mound of hay. She rolled, and then, fearful of being ambushed at any second, she popped up and looked back at the defeated outhouse.

She expected to see one very angry man in compromised attire quickly coming after her, but the outhouse appeared to be the only villain vanquished.

After hitting the ground, the outhouse had rolled over, pinning the door to the ground and its occupant inside. Loud shouting and cursing emitted from the fallen building. But all of the pounding didn't seem to be aiding any escape.

However, all of the ruckus he was making would soon draw the other men out of the shack, even if they were asleep. Jo didn't wait to see what happened, she didn't bother to make sure the outhouse hadn't inflicted injury, and she didn't waste any sympathy on whoever was trapped inside.

Instead, she ran.

Fear fueled her speed and she ran for a lot farther than she thought possible. She ran until her ribs felt like they were on fire, and still she kept going. Unfortunately, her boots couldn't kick up all the dirt to Perdition in a sprint.

Completely out of breath, she finally slowed. She wanted to stop altogether, bend over, and catch her breath, but she knew she had to at least continue walking until she could run again. The Pruitt men would come after her, of that she had no doubt.

She sent quick looks over her shoulder, even though she knew she should still have a few minutes before her abductors appeared. Either Elmer or Clyde was stuck in the outhouse. After getting him out, the men would still need to hitch up the horses to the wagon.

Jo told herself that with all that, she should have enough time to make it to Perdition. But the truth was, she had no idea how far away it was. Her trip in the wagon had been so disorienting that she didn't have a realistic recollection of how long it had taken to arrive at the Pruitt's place. And now, it appeared that the Pruitt shack and its unfortunate outbuildings were much farther out of town than Jo had estimated. Though she tried to stay positive, the horizon revealed no sign of the forlorn buildings of Perdition.

Jo walked as fast as she could, but as time passed, her anxiety only increased. She wasn't going fast enough. She knew the Pruitts would show up at any time, and she would be back just as abducted as she was before her encounters with the shed and outhouse.

Jo tried to come up with a plan that involved hiding if she heard them coming down the road. But without trees or bushes along the road, there weren't many hiding options. In fact, the landscape was so barren, there were actually *no* hiding options.

Jo was thirsty, tired, and she hurt from her feet to her head. If, by chance, the Pruitts didn't come after her, evening was fast approaching. Even now, the sun was sending streaks of colored lights across the sky in its daily finale. Jo didn't think she would make it to town in time. She would soon be caught out in the middle of a dark Texas night.

Despair threatened to overtake her. Just when she thought she might let it, movement caught her eye.

Forcing herself to keep walking, she shaded her eyes from the descending sun and strained to see up the road. She'd heard that one's mind could play tricks, but it really seemed like whatever she saw was getting larger, coming closer.

Jo quickened her step. If someone was coming from town, she could beg them for help. Maybe they would give her a ride back to Perdition. Of course, she didn't know what she would do once she got there, but she'd figure that out later. Right now, her goal was any added distance away from Oscar Pruitt.

There was definitely something coming down the road toward her, but Jo couldn't yet identify what the figure was. And she still wasn't sure if what she was seeing was real or just a mirage. She knew she was exhausted and desperate; she really wanted to believe that help was coming to meet her. Maybe this was the angel she prayed for!

The figure was close enough now for Jo to see that it was a horse and rider. Jo's feet began to move faster. Then, eager to meet her rescuer, she broke into a run, relief causing her to stumble in her haste.

Suddenly, she stopped. While she ran one second, the next her feet were ramrod straight and refusing to move, just as her mind refused to accept what her eyes were telling her.

The horse and rider pulled up, stopping right in front of her.

Jo's mouth fell open in shock.

Her rescuer was not a mirage, nor was he of heavenly origin.

Her eyes met a pair of familiar blue eyes.

Jo swallowed. *This isn't exactly what I meant, God!*

Though he may have been sent by God, Pete Harding was definitely no angel!

"What are you doing here?" Jo asked a bit sharper than she intended. She had, after all, prayed for help. She had even said she wouldn't turn help away. She just wasn't expecting it to come from the man who only last night rejected her!

Pete slid from the saddle, layers of dust coating his shirt and buckskin trousers and somehow making his intense blue eyes stand out even brighter. "I heard you might be in need of some rescuing," he said softly.

"Well, you heard wrong," Jo snapped. "As you can see, I can take care of myself."

Pete was silent while he gave her a thorough inspection from the tip of her mussed hair, to her ragged and filthy boots. "From where I am standing, you look a little rough for wear." Pete reached for her left hand, his eyes locking onto the angry rope burns that encircled her wrists.

"Then perhaps you shouldn't be standing here!" Jo bit out, deftly evading his grasp and crossing her arms to prevent further perusal.

Immediately realizing how she sounded, Jo quickly bit her tongue. What was she doing! Was she crazy? "I didn't mean that," she sighed, closing her eyes and trying to gather her harried thoughts. The truth is, I do need help. And I'm glad you're here."

"Me too."

Jo's gaze flew to Pete. His blue eyes burned brightly with raw emotion. Jo didn't dare to guess what it might be. She was still too hurt from yesterday to hope that his appearance here in Perdition might mean his feelings had changed.

"Jo, please let me see your hands," he said, cautiously reaching out his hand for hers.

Jo tried to dodge him, but this time, he wouldn't be deterred. He gently tugged her forearm until she allowed him access to her hand.

Jo watched as a muscle in Pete's jaw clenched.

"Did Pruitt do this to you?" Despite his obvious anger, Pete tenderly stroked her raw wrist.

"Yes, he and his sons. They kidnapped me."

"Amelia was right then."

Jo's eyes flew wide. "You saw Amelia? How is she? Are the rest of the girls safe?"

"Yes, they are in Perdition. Amelia saw me ride in and told me what happened."

Jo bit her lip, reluctant to make a full confession. She looked down at her boot and drew a circle in the dirt with the toe.

Pete held his silence, as if waiting for her report.

Sighing, she looked back up. "You were right," she resolutely admitted. Better to get it over with, even if that did require giving Pete Harding credit. "The agency that arranged the contracts was not legitimate. At least, my contract was a farce." She certainly hoped the other brides had fared better than she had.

Realizing that Pete's "rescue" was taking too much time, she glanced nervously over her shoulder. "Oscar Pruitt isn't who he claimed to be. He lied. And we don't have much time. I'm sure Pruitt and his sons will be along soon. They didn't exactly let me go. I escaped."

Pete smiled. "Of course you did. You are a fighter. That's one of the things I love about you."

Jo froze, her breath catching in her throat. "Love?" she whispered. Had she heard him correctly?

Pete took her right hand and laced her fingers with his own. Bringing their joined hands to his mouth, he gently brushed his lips across her knuckles.

His eyes looked back up to claim hers. Honesty shown like blue flames. "Yes, Josephine Franklin," he said firmly. "I love you. I was a fool to let you believe any different last night. I couldn't get my lips to speak my heart, and I let you think I didn't want to marry you. The truth is that I do want to marry you, but not for convenience or fear of regret. I want you to be my wife simply because I'm completely, can't-think-straight, heart-making-a-ruckus, in love with you. I just hope I am not too late."

Jo was so shocked she couldn't feel her body. She moved her lips to respond, but no sound came out.

As if eager to continue before losing his nerve, Pete hurried to explain. "I've loved you since I first saw you at the train that night. Your passion and strength was evident even though it was dark as a pail, and you were covered from head to foot in manure. I tried to keep away from you, to push you away, but I couldn't help myself. I fell in love with you more each day. And then I let you go."

Pete paused, his eyes searching Jo's. "I've made many mistakes in my life, lived a life more full of regrets than anything else. But, at the moment, the biggest regret I have is that I let you walk away from me last night without doing this."

Pete slowly lowered himself to one knee, his eyes never leaving Jo's face. "I love you more than there are stars in this big Texas sky, Jo. I don't want to live in the past anymore. I want a future with you. If you will have me, I would like you to be my wife. Because I love you. Will you marry me, Josephine?"

Jo tried to tamper the tears rolling down her cheeks, but a happy sob escaped. "Yes, Peter, I will marry you."

Pete rose quickly, crushing Jo to his broad chest, and showering her with kisses to her forehead and cheeks before claiming her lips for his own.

His lips on her were firm and spoke of a passion that Jo had never known. His kiss wasn't demanding, but it wasn't gentle either. It left no doubt that this man loved her deeply and would as long as he lived.

Jo didn't think a person could exist without breathing, but she wasn't sure she had ever existed before kissing Pete. She felt faint from lack of breath, and yet she felt more alive than she had in her entire life.

After several moments, Jo drew back, desperately gulping in air.

"When will you marry me?" Pete asked, his voice gravelly.

"Just as soon as we hop on your horse and outrun my fiancé," Jo answered quickly, looking back down the road and expecting to see a trio of filthy Pruitts.

Pete's brows lowered. "I don't plan on runnin' from those

skunks. Me and Oscar Pruitt need to have a little talk about how he has treated you."

Jo instantly panicked. "No, Pete, please! I don't want to ever see Oscar Pruitt or his sons again. Please take me back to Perdition!"

Though Pete was still reluctant to go, he allowed Jo to lead him toward the waiting horse.

"Besides," Jo said eagerly, "I am worried about Amelia, Sadie, and Meg. I will feel better when I see that they are safe with my own eyes."

What Jo didn't say is that she was also still afraid of what would happen if the Pruitts did catch up to her. Could Pete protect her when Oscar had a signed document saying she agreed to be his wife? She shuddered to think of what he would do if he couldn't save her from those men. She didn't want him hurt.

Pete looked over her shoulder, his gaze searching the horizon. Jo was afraid to turn. She feared that her eyes would find a cloud of dust heralding the arrival of the Pruitts.

"Sun is going down. I 'spose we can head back to Perdition tonight," Pete's eyes sparkled as he tossed her a sly grin. "Did you really mean it when you said you would marry me if we outran the Pruitts?"

"Well, yes, I suppose." Jo said confusedly, not sure where Pete was headed with his question.

"I'm going to hold you to that." And with that, Pete gently lifted Jo into the saddle, clearly remembering her bruised ribs. Once she was settled, he swung up behind her, deftly holding the reigns and turning the stallion toward Perdition and away from Jo's nightmare.

"I just happened to see that there was a wedding goin' on at the church when I flew by there. That means the preacher is in town." Pete grinned. "Do you regret promisin' me now?"

Jo tilted her head back to see him better. "No regrets... ever." She smiled, as she leaned further into his embrace. "I do have a question though. How did you make it so quickly from Last Chance? Since they were still finishing repairs along the track, I didn't think there was another train today."

"You ever hear that the shortest distance between two points is a straight line? I didn't take the train. I took a horse and didn't exactly follow the train tracks. It isn't an easy ride, which is why the train is a much better, much faster option. I came to my senses right after you left, but I got delayed and missed the train leaving Last Chance. It took me over eight hours to get here, and that's probably a record for that trail. I put my poor horse through a lot trying to make it here in time to stop you from marrying Pruitt. Speaking of horses, I hope you don't mind making a stop before heading to the church. Otherwise, you might find yourself married to a horse thief."

"You stole this horse?"

"More like borrowed...without permission," Pete grinned mischievously. "My horse made it, but he was so worn out, I had to switch mounts in Perdition. Don't worry. I only took this horse from a friend. He just wasn't home at the time. We should be safe. I didn't gallop across half of Texas to marry you and then end up at the gallows."

Pete kissed her head. "But to be truthful, I made it here so quickly, because I prayed. Every mile."

"You weren't the only one praying," Jo said softly. "When I was locked in that shed trying to get out—"

"Wait, they tied you up and locked you in a shed?"

"Yes."

Pete sharply reined in the horse and spun him around. "Perhaps I will end up in the gallows after all."

"No, Pete!" Jo cried, stilling his hands that held the reigns. "I'm fine. I climbed up onto the roof, jumped onto the outhouse and rode it to the ground as it toppled over."

A dark brow rose as Pete cracked a slight smile. "I'm glad you escaped, and so inventively I might add, but that doesn't make up for the fact that those men need to be held accountable for takin' you against your will in the first place."

Jo shrugged. "If it makes you feel any better, one of the Pruitts was stuck inside the outhouse at the time,"

Pete stared at her incredulously before tilting his head back and letting out a bark of laughter. Still chuckling, he turned the horse back toward town. "That's my Josephine. I could almost feel sorry for those men if I didn't want to kill them. They had no idea they tried to cage a wildcat."

Jo adopted a pout. "There you go, Pete Harding, comparing me to animals. If you ever want your lucky fish hook back, you are going to have to show better manners!"

"I don't need my lucky fish hook anymore. I'm the luckiest fisherman in the world. I caught you."

Jo felt her cheeks warm. "You certainly did. And I have a bald spot to prove it."

"You don't have a bald spot. You're perfect. Don't forget, I've seen you... all of you."

Jo's cheeks ignited to a forest fire. Even if it wasn't true, her future husband definitely knew how to get her riled, which should make marriage to him a lot of fun!

Deciding to play along, Jo put a finger to her lips. "Shhhh! Pete Harding, you are supposed to forget that ever happened. I demand it."

"No can do," Pete shook his head. "Best fishin' day of my life."

Pete

Perdition, Texas

"And do you, Peter Harding, take this woman to be your lawful wife? To love and to cherish. In sickness and in health, as long as you both shall live?"

Pete gazed into the eyes of his bride, hardly believing that he was so blessed to be here in a moment he thought would never happen. He swallowed, and answered in a firm voice that contained no waver, "I do."

The preacher turned to Jo. "And do you, Josephine Franklin, take this man to be your lawful husband? To love and to cherish. In sickness and in health, as long as you both shall live?"

"I do." Jo's voice rang clear and strong.

Pete felt a burning behind his eyes and tried to keep his emotion under control. After losing Isobel, Pete thought he would never hear a woman say those words. In fact, he hadn't wanted it to happen. But, despite his aversion to women as a species, Jo had charged into his heart.

And still, he had almost let her walk away. After nearly repeating the same mistake of remaining silent about how he felt, he had realized something stronger than regret.

Love.

He relinquished his past to the only One who could redeem him from the guilt and bitterness, letting his love for Jo heal his heart and give him the courage to chase after a future with Jo and speak his heart.

The minister mopped his brow with a handkerchief and spoke, "Then I now pronounce you husband and wife. You may—"

"Now hold on a doggone minute!" A loud voice boomed from the back of the empty church. "That's my wife he's tryin' to marry! I paid for her myself!"

Pete felt Jo stiffen beside him. His eyes narrowed and he turned, positioning himself in front of Jo. The trio of men strode up the aisle toward where he and Jo stood with the preacher. But Pete was ready.

"Now this is what I'm talking about," said George, the roughened cowboy who had volunteered to be their witness. He gleefully rubbed his dirty hands together. I'm thinkin' I owe you a little payback, Oscar." He sidled a glance Pete's direction, "Let's take 'em, Pete."

"She is not your wife, Pruitt," Pete said, his voice low and dangerous. His fists clenched at his sides with his fingers itching to punish Oscar Pruitt for his treatment of Jo. If Pete had his way, he would return tenfold the damage Pruitt had inflicted upon the woman he loved.

"She is so!" Pruitt insisted. "I have the paper to prove it. She belongs to me!"

Jo's soft hands at Pete's arms held him back, and Pete worked to keep himself in check. This was Jo's wedding, and she deserved good memories. Knocking out Oscar Pruitt might make for fond memories for him, but he didn't think the same would be true for Jo.

"Listen," Pete said calmly. "I will reimburse you for any money you have spent on *my* wife's travel."

Pete reached for his wallet in his trousers.

"I'm not interested in your money." Oscar weaved unsteadily between his two sons. The raw smell of alcohol as well as another strong odor permeated the room. Was that sewage?

Pete spared a glance at the burly son. Sure enough, dark stains and the putrid stench clung heavily to his clothes and skin.

I guess we know who must have been the unfortunate occupant of that outhouse Jo rode, Pete thought smugly. Though he realized that with a pit beneath an outhouse, upending the building itself shouldn't have such a smelly result, he was pleased enough with the misfortune to not waste time speculating on how it happened.

Turning back, Pete tried again. For Jo's sake. "Listen, Pruitt, how much did you pay? I will double it. Take the money and go."

"I'm not goin' anywhere without that woman. She's mine. I have a contract that says she's my wife."

"You have a fake contract," Jo spoke up from behind Pete.

"Just like I was sent a fake letter for a fake arrangement. Besides, it's null and void now anyway. I'm already married. To him." Jo laced her fingers with Pete's.

A vein on Oscar's forehead sprung to life. "Now you hush up, woman! Yer mine. And yer comin' with me!" Oscar reached past Pete and grabbed Jo's shoulder.

Pete quickly knocked Oscar's hand away.

"Well, I tried." Pete said with a sigh. With that, Pete pulled back his fist and punched Oscar directly in the jaw.

Oscar's eyes rolled back into his head and he fell to the church floor like a pail full of pig slop.

"Hey, that's our pa! Yer goin' to regret that!"

The thinner Pruitt son rushed Pete, closely followed by his bigger, smellier brother.

Pete dodged one punch and followed with a left hook of his own. His fist connected with Skinny Pruitt's nose.

Pete didn't pause. He swiftly turned his body, making sure Jo was still safely behind him before sending a kick into the ribs of the one who could only be referred to as Stinky Pruitt.

Stinky bent over, clutching his stomach.

Pete would have punched him as well, but a boot was about as close as he wanted to get to the filth on the man.

Pete turned just in time to see Skinny Pruitt, blood streaming from his broken nose, launch himself at Pete.

Pete sidestepped, and Skinny fell on top of his pa who was just beginning to rouse.

"What is going on in here?" A young man with brown hair and a silver badge pinned to his black vest rushed into the church, followed quickly by a woman Pete immediately recognized.

"Oh, Jo, are you okay?" Amelia asked, dashing to Jo's side.

"I've been so worried about you!"

"Sheriff, arrest this man," Oscar Pruitt jabbed a finger toward Pete as he stumbled to his feet. "He's trying to steal my wife."

"Are you sure about that, Oscar?" The sheriff asked, casually leaning against the first pew. "I've been hearing a much different story from a very sincere and reliable witness. The way I hear it, you and your sons kidnapped this woman, tying her hands up, putting a gag in her mouth, and throwing her in the back of your wagon."

They had gagged Jo too! Pete's blood boiled. He pulled his fist back ready to clock Pruitt again, but Jo grabbed his hand back.

"That's plain not true, Sheriff. I have a contract and everything. It's here somewhere." Oscar patted down his worn jacket, searching its pockets.

"I don't know about any contracts, but I do know that taking a woman against her will can get you thrown in jail," the sheriff said. Turning to Jo, he asked, "Did these men kidnap you, miss?"

"It's missus actually," Jo replied, holding Pete's hand tightly. "Mrs. Harding. And yes, they did."

"You kidnapped a married woman?" the sheriff asked incredulously. "No wonder her husband punched you. I think you boys best come down to the office with me. You might need to take this up with the circuit judge."

"Well, now, Sheriff, I think we just had ourselves a misunderstanding. Me and the boys meant no harm to her. We would have brought her back..."

"We will see about that," the sheriff said, shaking his head. "Oscar and Clyde, you come with me. Elmer, I'm going to excuse you for the moment. I don't know what you got into, but I can't have you stinkin' up the jail."

"He was in the outhouse when it tipped over," Skinny Pruitt reported helpfully.

"What kind of outhouse do you Pruitts have?" the sheriff asked, thoroughly confused. "The only way he could get that stinky is if he went bathing in the pit, not the outhouse!"

"Well, he kinda did!" Skinny said sheepishly.

Oscar cleared his throat. "We were a bit anxious to help Elmer. I guess we righted the outhouse with a little too much strength."

"Or too much whiskey," Stinky growled, glaring at his father and brother.

Skinny continued, a bit remorseful. "The bottom broke as soon as it was upright, and Elmer plumb fell into the pit!"

Pete snorted, working hard to control his laughter. He didn't want to make things worse when it looked like the sheriff was handling things.

"That must be some pit," the sheriff said seriously.

"It is," Skinny confirmed. "Can't quite remember why we made the fool thing so big. I'm sure there was a good reason at the time."

"There was," Stinky grumbled. "Too much whiskey."

Oscar glared at his son.

Stinky glared back. "Same problem you had when you gave all our money for this fool woman! Now look at us. I may stink, but I'm thinkin' you're the one who is stinkin' rotten!"

Oscar growled and threw an unsteady punch at his son, but Stinky ducked. Whereas Oscar and Skinny seemed more than a little tipsy, a dunk in the outhouse pit appeared to have sobered Stinky up. He lunged back at Oscar, but the sheriff pulled the older man out of the way and put up his hands.

"Hold on there, Elmer!" the sheriff said, clearly trying to calm the situation without actually getting close enough to restrain Stinky. "Elmer, I'm sure you can locate a horse trough or something to get cleaned up in. I'd suggest burning your clothes."

The sheriff turned to the preacher, "Reverend Gates, please continue. I think you have a wedding to complete."

With a wink toward Amelia, the sheriff led the Pruitt men back down the aisle.

"Well, where was I?" Reverend Gates asked, clutching his Bible. "I think I may have lost my train of thought."

"I think we were at the kissing part, Reverend," Pete said, smiling down at Jo.

"Well, then, you may kiss your bride."

"I believe I will." Pete lowered his lips to Jo's, relishing in their softness.

Clapping from Amelia and whistles from George finally made him draw away.

Gazing into Jo's eyes, Pete silently thanked the Lord for all of His mercies and grace. Clasping her hand in his, he moved to lead her down the aisle. It was dark out now and too late to head back to Last Chance tonight. Instead, they would have a nice dinner and stay in the Perdition hotel. Then they would ride the train loop back around to Last Chance tomorrow. He would not take his wife back the way he'd come. That ride was much too rough. He was sure his horse would also appreciate a ride back home in a train car.

He clasped Jo's hand tighter, his heart thumping at the thought of taking his wife back home to stay. This was one woman who definitely belonged on a ranch—his ranch.

"We'll catch the first train back home tomorrow," he told his new wife as they walked down the aisle. "Josh and Addie are going to need some help since Addie is laid up with the birth."

"What do you mean?" Jo asked, her eyes flying wide open. "Addie had her baby? Today?"

Pete grinned. "I said I was delayed, remember? I sent for the doctor right after Josh left with you ladies. Addie said something about water breaking, but I didn't ask for any details. Then we had to wait for a good two hours for Josh to get back from the train. He barely made it. I heard a baby cry right after Josh rushed upstairs."

Jo squealed in delight. "That was fast! I can't wait! Did she have a boy or a girl?"

Pete quirked an eyebrow. "Not sayin'. Addie made me promise not to tell. She told me to bring you back to meet your new niece or nephew."

Jo pouted. "And there are no more trains tonight?" Then, as if struck by an idea, she looked up at Pete and fluttered her eyelashes. "Well, maybe I can find a way to convince you to tell."

Pete grinned. "You are more than welcome to try, Mrs. Harding. But if I go back on Addie's orders, I'm sure I will live to regret it!"

Pete held the church door open for Jo, and they exited onto the porch that overlooked the buildings of Perdition. Night had fallen with lights from the hotel and saloon illuminating the shadowing hulks of the town.

In the light from the church, he looked down at his beautiful bride.

Jo tilted her head to the side to look up at him, the teasing light in her eye turning serious. "*Do* you have any regrets, Mr. Harding?"

At her words, he paused, knowing her question was more

than simple words. His mind automatically flashing back to his brother... and Isobel. But somehow, their memories didn't quite carry the same sting that had plagued him for so many years. He had asked the Lord for forgiveness, and he knew, down to his bones, that it had been given. More than that, love from Jo and for Jo had somehow healed the bitterness and hurt, allowing him to move on to a future where the memories of his past mistakes were left as tools in God's hands and no longer held condemnation.

Movement caught his eye. Pete looked up from his thoughts to see the shadows of a handcuffed and still-protesting Oscar Pruitt being prodded down the darkened street by the sheriff. Oscar shot Pete one last angry look, giving him a full view of his cherry red cheek—the imprint of Pete's fist still clearly visible.

Pete smiled as he gently tugged Jo into his arms once again. Bending, he whispered in her ear, "Regrets? Not a one."

Author's Note

We love using actual history when writing our books because, often, reality is so much better than any imagination can dream up. This book begins with a train derailment caused by a manure slide, which sounds quite amusing. But what makes it even better is that the premise is actually based in fact.

At the close of the 19th century the world had a big problem—manure. Work and transportation depended on animals, but those animals came with a great deal of waste. With a single horse producing 15 to 35 pounds of manure a day, imagine how much a large city would need to deal with! It was such a big concern that in, 1894, a London newspaper wrote an article predicting that the city would eventually be buried under manure! Accordingly, the issue was soon dubbed the "Great Horse Manure Crisis of 1894." It was a big deal! Cities even held meetings trying to brainstorm solutions, but all to no avail.

In the end, the issue was resolved by what some may term

a miracle. With one invention, the world was forever saved from the threat of excess manure.

Hello, automobile.

Yes, with the invention of the car, what had been an insurmountable problem quickly became obsolete. Afterward, mentioning the "Great Horse Manure Crisis of 1894" was used as an encouragement not to worry. Even if a problem seems impossible, something will always show up.

In our book, we felt it appropriate that the liveryman, George, have his own solution for the manure problem in Last Chance. After all, it needed to be disposed of in some way. But in George's case, a lot of rain mixed with his solution didn't end well!

We hope you enjoyed that scene as well as the entire book. And now we leave you with the hope that all of your problems be on par with the "Great Horse Manure Crisis of 1894." May your automobile soon make its appearance!

P.S. If you want to know more about this historical event, here is a short article that includes details mentioned here. Enjoy!

Http://www.historic-uk.com/HistoryUK/HistoryofBritain/Great-Horse-Manure-Crisis-of-1894/

ENJOY this sneak peek at, ***Bride by Default***, book 1 in the ***Brides of Perdition*** series coming soon.

Perdition, Texas–1881

"Sadie, something isn't right."

"I know, Amelia," Sadie Riggins said, watching their friend and fellow mail-order-bride, Jo Franklin, disappear out the train depot doors. "There's something mighty fishy going on here. And I didn't like the look of that George fellow."

Turning to the station master, Sadie leaned over the counter. "Who is this Oscar Pruitt exactly? And why does the mention of his name make you look like a cat that just got its tail slammed in the back door? Is our friend in any danger?"

"Well, I don't know that he is dangerous, Miss," the station master said, rubbing his spectacles nervously on his black vest. "But he certainly isn't a man I would think genteel ladies like yourselves would want to be associated with."

"That doesn't sound good," Meg moaned. "What are we going to do?"

"Where was that George fellow headed?" Sadie asked.

"The saloon I expect. Oscar Pruitt and his sons can always be found at the Cattle Prod this time of day. They don't usually head back to their shack until closing time."

"Shack?!" Meg screeched in alarm. "Jo thought she was marrying a rancher! Oh, Sadie, we need to help her!"

"And we will," Sadie said confidently, pushing up the sleeves of her dress to her elbows, and securing a few wayward strands of chestnut hair back into her bun. "Come on, girls. Let's go teach this Oscar fellow that he doesn't mess with mail-order brides."

"Sadie, wait," Amelia grabbed her arm, stopping her march toward the depot doors. "Don't you think we should find some help before we rush into a saloon by ourselves?"

Sadie tilted her head back and laughed. "Oh, Amelia, I have six older brothers. I think I can handle one Mr. Oscar Pruitt."

"But didn't the station master say something about him having sons?" Meg asked twisting her lace handkerchief between her gloved fingers.

"Yes," the older man nodded empathically, "two of the meanest, ugliest fellows you ever did see."

"Well, you haven't met my oldest brother, Aaron," Sadie said confidently. "But alright, Amelia, we can do this your way. What 'help' do you have in mind?"

"Perhaps if we located yours or Meg's grooms, they could be of assistance."

"Why not yours?" Sadie asked directly. A quick flash of emotion sparked in Amelia's eyes, but it was gone before Sadie could define what it meant. Ever since they had met on the train to Texas, Amelia had been very tight-lipped, rarely speaking, and never about herself. The other three mail-order brides had shared tidbits of their pasts and their fiancés, who they were meeting in Perdition. But not Amelia. Sadie was more than a little curious.

"Someone needs to find the Sheriff," Amelia said, clearly avoiding Sadie's question. "I can do that while you find your fiancé."

Sadie looked at Amelia for several moments before slowly nodding and turning back to the station master. "Okay, Mister, where can I find Lionel Faraday?"

Once again, the man seemed to struggle for words. "Lionel Faraday, you said?"

"Yep. That's him," Sadie hoped her voice didn't reflect the worry that suddenly gripped her heart. The station master appeared to be even more shocked than when Jo had announced her fiancé's name.

What have I gotten myself into? Sadie thought uneasily. But as soon as the question raised itself, she pushed it out of her mind. Well, there's no backing down now. I am NOT going back to Boston and prove my brothers right!

Sadie's six brothers had all voiced their disapproval of her plan to become a mail-order bride. But she stubbornly stuck to her guns, and let the Irish temper that she inherited from her mother rear its red head.

The way Sadie saw it, she was going to end up a spinster if she stayed in Boston. Her brothers were merciless with any gentlemen who even looked in Sadie's direction. It was because of them that she had never had a beau or been courted. Every man who approached her quickly found a wall of six burly Irishmen standing between him and Sadie Riggins.

Shaking off her worry, Sadie asked the station master again, "Do you know where he is?"

"Well, yes, Miss. He's at the church."

Sadie let out a huge sigh of relief. "The church? Well, isn't that wonderful!" Sadie beamed at Meg and Amelia. "My fiancé is at the church. I have to admit that I was worried for a second. Especially after Jo's fiancé looks like he is a yellow-bellied liar. But Lionel Faraday is obviously the good, Christian man that he claimed to be."

"Oh," Sadie clapped her hands excitedly. "I'll bet he is talking to the preacher about our wedding!"

"Well, I think there is some wedding talk going on," the station master said hesitantly, but Sadie paid him no heed. She was already headed toward the door.

"Come on, Meg," Sadie ordered. "You can come with me while Amelia finds the sheriff."

Then, not even turning around to address the station master, she called over her shoulder, "Thanks for your help, Mister. We will be back for our trunks."

Once she was outside the depot, Sadie shaded her eyes and looked at the few buildings that haphazardly lined the dirt street of Perdition, Texas.

"There," she said excitedly, pointing to a white-washed

building topped with a brown wooden cross. "That must be the church. I'll hurry on over there with Meg, and we will meet back here to re-group. Sound good, Amelia?"

"Yes, let's just hurry. I'm worried about Jo."

"Me too. And my fists are just itchin' to wallop that Oscar." Sadie set off down the street with Meg running to catch up.

"I hope you don't mean to hit him, Sadie," Meg said breathlessly. "Ladies really shouldn't punch people."

Sadie laughed. "Do you have any brothers, Meg?"

"Well, no," Meg admitted. "I have no siblings."

"With six brothers, a girl has to learn some survival skills. I am not ashamed to admit this lady has been known to throw a punch or two." After practically sprinting down the street and up a short rise, Sadie raced up the church steps with Meg panting in her wake.

She clasped the handles on each of the double doors, eagerly urging, . "Come on, Meg, let's meet the man I'm going to marry!"

With a determined jerk, Sadie opened both doors at once.

Startled gasps filled the room.

Sadie's mouth dropped in surprise.

The church was filled with people. Every pew was fully occupied, and all eyes were now on Sadie and Meg.

"Is today Sunday?" Sadie asked loudly. "I thought for sure it was Saturday."

"No, Sadie," Meg whispered urgently in her ear. "Look at the front."

Sadie's eyes raced up the aisle to where a man and woman stood holding hands in front of the preacher.

"I'm so sorry," Sadie stuttered, feeling the immediate urge to escape. She wasn't the type to blush in embarrassment, but she did feel horrible for interrupting this poor couple's special day. "Forgive me for interrupting. I didn't realize that a wedding was being held."

Quickly, she grabbed Meg's arm and towed her to the nearest pew. If they could just sit down a moment, the wedding would continue and Sadie could locate her groom directly afterward.

"Excuse me," she whispered loudly, making her way to a few inches of space in the middle of the last pew.

Meg, her face flaming with mortification, whispered hoarsely, "Sadie, I don't think we should—"

"Excuse me," she whispered again. And again.

Punctuating every two seconds with a polite "excuse me" for every time she bumped into the knees of the pew's occupants, she wriggled a path while keeping firm hold of Meg.

With a strangled gasp, Meg nearly fell into the lap of a bearded gentleman.

Frustrated, Sadie paused. This plan was obviously not working. In her efforts at subtlety, she was drawing more attention, not less. Letting out her breath in exasperation, she gave up and turned her eyes to the minister.

"I'm so sorry, but I was told that I could find my fiancé here. I'm looking for Lionel Faraday."

Another round of shocked gasps filled the room.

A woman with white hair rose regally from the front pew. Turning, she marched purposely down the aisle toward Sadie and Meg, her frosty eyes shooting sparks that let Sadie know in no uncertain terms that trouble was a-coming.

"Frank, would you kindly escort these ladies out of the church?" the woman said kindly, though her eyes pinned Sadie with a glare. "I'm sure they will need to catch a train back from where they came."

"Yes, ma'am." An ample man beside Sadie's elbow popped up and began herding them back from the pew to the aisle.

Sadie sputtered, not knowing what to do. By the look on this woman's face, Sadie knew this wasn't a friendly relocation so they could speak in privacy. She and Meg were being thrown out of the church.

"Excuse me," she managed, trying to stall as she was literally being pushed toward the door from behind. "Just who are you? And where is my betrothed?"

The white-haired woman stepped forward, stopping inches from Sadie, dislike radiating off of her in waves. "My name is Jean Faraday, and I'm afraid you are mistaken. You are not Lionel Faraday's fiancée."

Sadie's green eyes flashed and her chin rose. "And why not?"

"Because that is his wife standing next to him at the front. They were just married. And you, my dear, are too late."

IF you enjoyed ***Bride of Pretense*** by Cami Wesley and Amanda Tru, be sure to check these additional titles which are sure to please.

The Brides by Mail Series by Cami Wesley and Amanda Tru:

Book 1: Bride of Pretense

Book 2: Bride by Request

Book 2: Bride of Regret

The Tru Exceptions Series by Amanda Tru:

Book 1: Baggage Claim

Book 2: Point of Origin

Book 3: Mirage

Stand-Alone Novels by Amanda Tru:

Secret Santa

The Romance of the Sugar Plum Fairy

Random Acts of Cupid

The Assumption of Guilt

Proudly published by *Walker Hammond Publishers.*

YESTERDAY SERIES

ALL six thrilling tales of time-travel in Amanda Tru's best-selling saga, the **Yesterday Series**, are available now in newly edited editions, complete with discussion questions for individuals or book clubs and all new timeline diagrams.

The Yesterday Series:

Book 1: Yesterday

Book 2: The Locket

Book 3: Today

Book 4: The Choice

Book 5: Tomorrow

Book 6: The Promise

Proudly presented by *Sign of the Whale Books*, a division of *Olivia Kimbrell Press.*

Discussion Questions

Isn't it wonderful that God is in charge and not us? If we were really in control, it would be far too easy to screw things up. In our limited vision, we can see only a portion of our story; whereas God can see the whole thing—from beginning to end. He can redeem our mistakes and miraculously transform even the darkest of times into something to our benefit.

Pete was never meant to be a main character. When we first introduced him in book 1, we had no idea that he would need his own book. But when we outlined Pete's backstory, we realized we couldn't leave him as he was. We had to show his redemption and give him a resolution for his tragedy and regret. As in everything, God had a plan for Pete, even though we didn't know it when we first imagined him!

The message of this book and Pete's life deals with regrets. No one can make it through life without experiencing mistakes or wishing they had handled something differently. Getting past those mistakes and dealing with the tragedies that come can be difficult for anyone. While we wanted to give a realistic portrayal of guilt and grief, we also wanted to show a clear message of how to live life without regrets.

It is our hope that the following questions take you for a deeper journey through this oft-times humorous story. May they prompt you to study how God would have you live, and give you hope that regrets can be tools in God's hands for your ultimate good. May you truly join Pete in saying "Regrets? No, not a one."

After all, God already has them covered.

The opening scene of this book is a tragic one where we fully see the pain Pete has experienced and feel his grief and guilt. While Pete recognizes that he should have handled things differently, he feels helpless. Helpless to change the past and helpless to combat his intense feelings.

1. Have you ever experienced something you wish you had handled differently? What was it? Did your emotions interfere with how you handled the situation? Did you feel guilt and regret as Pete did?

   2 Samuel 24:10

2. Pete's actions had consequences not only for himself, but for others. How did his actions affect the people he cared about?

   Matthew 27:3-4, Hebrews 12:14-15

3. What is bitterness?

   Proverbs 15:13, Leviticus 19:18

4. Have you ever felt bitter or witnessed bitterness in someone else? Did the bitterness come with consequences? How did it affect others?

   Ephesians 4:26, Matthew 6:14-15

A significant part of Pete's regret resulted from anger toward himself—so much so that he struggled with forgiving himself.

5. Have you ever felt angry at yourself? How did you handle it? Were you able to find forgiveness?

   Matthew 26:75

In some ways, Jo contrasts Pete. She was not treated fairly by her husband's family, yet her past has not made her bitter.

6. Tell of a time where you or someone you cared about was treated unfairly. How did you react? Were you more like Pete or Jo?

   Ephesians 4:31-32, James 1:19-20

7. Everyone has difficult times in life. Tell of a time when you experienced something that could have made you bitter and did not. How were you able to deal with it in a healthy way?

John 16:33, Colossians 3:12-14, Proverbs 10:12

Neither Pete nor Jo are perfect characters, which makes some fun reading!

8. What do you think are their strengths? Weaknesses? Do you relate more to Pete or Jo?

9. Pete almost repeats his mistakes and let his emotions cause him to lose someone he cared about. What changed for him?

10. How do you see God working in Jo's life? How did both Pete and Jo need to change in order to bring them together?

11. What has God been working with you on?

Philippians 1:6

When Jo was trapped in the shed, she prayed for rescue. But it came in a form she didn't expect--Pete.

12. Tell of a time when God answered your prayer in a way you didn't expect? Did God's plan turn out better than your own?

    Romans 8:28, Proverbs 16:9

While this book covered a lot of heavy issues, it was tempered with a good deal of humor.

13. What did you appreciate most? What was your favorite part?

14. What is your recipe for living without regrets?

    Jeremiah 29:11, Philippians 2:13, Romans 12:17-21

If you are doing this Bible Study with a group, please discuss what you can pray with each other about and join together in prayer.

NOTES:

_____

_____

_____

_____

_____

_____

_____

_____

_____

_____

_____

_____

About the Authors

Amanda Tru and **Cami Wesley** are sisters, best friends, and a dynamic writing team! Growing up, Amanda and Cami fought over who got to read books first and dreamed of being authors.

Amanda got her start first, and is the author of more than sixteen books under her own name. Finally convincing her sister to write with her, they wrote *Bride of Pretense* together, never imagining how much fun it would be to mix history, humor, and their Christian faith to develop a unique story and write every scene together. They now believe the most fun way to write is together and feel they bring out the best in each other. Of course, making each other cry with laughter along the way is an added bonus!

Amanda is a busy mom of four young children and lives in Idaho. Cami is an equally busy mom of three children and also lives in Idaho.

Both get their writing done at night, sacrificing sleep and a clean house to write stories that let others have an excuse to get out of their own sleep and cleaning!

Connect Online

Author site:

http://amandatru.com/

Newsletter email sign up:

http://eepurl.com/ZQdw9

Facebook:

https://www.facebook.com/amandatru.author

https://www.facebook.com/pages/Cami-Wesley/1468705350116056

Twitter:

https://twitter.com/TruAmanda

GooglePlus+:

https://plus.google.com/+AmandaTru

Pinterest:

http://www.pinterest.com/truamanda/

Goodreads:

https://www.goodreads.com/author/show/5374686.Amanda_Tru